OLIVER
Oliver, Lin.
Almost identical /
33090022304549

P9-CAO-844

MAIN 01/13

LONG BEACH PUBLIC LIBRARY
101 PACIFIC AVE.
LONG BEACH, CA 90822

almost
identical

almost identical

by Lin Oliver

Grosset & Dunlap
An Imprint of Penguin Group (USA) Inc.

We gratefully acknowledge the
poem contributed by Sonya Sones,
author of *Stop Pretending* and other
young adult novels in verse.

GROSSET & DUNLAP
Published by the Penguin Group
Penguin Group (USA) Inc., 375 Hudson Street, New York, New York 10014, USA
Penguin Group (Canada), 90 Eglinton Avenue East, Suite 700,
Toronto, Ontario M4P 2Y3, Canada
(a division of Pearson Penguin Canada Inc.)
Penguin Books Ltd., 80 Strand, London WC2R 0RL, England
Penguin Group Ireland, 25 St. Stephen's Green, Dublin 2, Ireland
(a division of Penguin Books Ltd.)
Penguin Group (Australia), 250 Camberwell Road, Camberwell, Victoria 3124, Australia
(a division of Pearson Australia Group Pty. Ltd.)
Penguin Books India Pvt. Ltd., 11 Community Centre,
Panchsheel Park, New Delhi—110 017, India
Penguin Group (NZ), 67 Apollo Drive, Rosedale, Auckland 0632, New Zealand
(a division of Pearson New Zealand Ltd.)
Penguin Books (South Africa) (Pty.) Ltd., 24 Sturdee Avenue,
Rosebank, Johannesburg 2196, South Africa

Penguin Books Ltd., Registered Offices: 80 Strand, London WC2R 0RL, England

If you purchased this book without a cover, you should be aware that this book is stolen
property. It was reported as "unsold and destroyed" to the publisher, and neither the author nor
the publisher has received any payment for this "stripped book."

All rights reserved. No part of this book may be reproduced, scanned, or distributed in any
printed or electronic form without permission. Please do not participate in or encourage piracy
of copyrighted materials in violation of the author's rights. Purchase only authorized editions.

The publisher does not have any control over and does not assume any responsibility for
author or third-party websites or their content.

Cover illustration by Mallory Grigg.

Text copyright © 2012 by Lin Oliver. All rights reserved. Published by Grosset & Dunlap,
a division of Penguin Young Readers Group, 345 Hudson Street, New York, New York 10014.
GROSSET & DUNLAP is a trademark of Penguin Group (USA) Inc. Printed in the U.S.A.

Library of Congress Control Number: 2011043240

ISBN 978-0-448-45191-6 (pbk)   10 9 8 7 6 5 4 3 2 1
ISBN 978-0-448-45865-6 (hc)   10 9 8 7 6 5 4 3 2 1

ALWAYS LEARNING   PEARSON

33090022304549

*For Bonnie Bader, Lauren Roth,
and Allie Roth—who inspired this
book from start to finish!—LO*

The Weigh-In

....

Chapter 1

"Step up on the scale, young lady. Let's see what you weigh."

Dr. Hartley was leaning against the wall, holding my chart, and smiling like he had just said a normal thing. I'm sorry. That was about as not-normal a request as I've ever heard.

Are you totally insane? I thought. *Get on the scale? Right here? Right now? With everyone watching?*

I think we can all agree that asking a girl who is almost thirteen to hop on a scale and have her weight announced in public is seriously horrifying. Especially if the girl in question—and that would be me—has always felt too fat for her own good.

I was facing the big, stupid scale in the hallway of Dr. Hartley's office where my twin sister, Charlie, and

I were getting our yearly start-of-school checkups. My dad was hovering around me like he couldn't wait to see the results. (Which, by the way, he couldn't.) Our fourteen-year-old brother, Ryan, was lurking in the hall, too, pretending to drop off his pee sample on the green linoleum counter, but I knew he was just being his usual nosy self. And as if having my family clustered around weren't bad enough, also within earshot were two nurses, a receptionist, a whining four-year-old with a gross leg rash, his mother, and a random plumber who was checking out a leak underneath the sink.

I couldn't believe Dr. Hartley, my very own pediatrician, who was there when I was born, who wears a clip-on teddy bear on his stethoscope, who nuzzles babies and tells knock-knock jokes, actually wanted me to hop right up on the scale in front of—count 'em—*nine people!* Nine and a half if you count the four-year-old with the leg rash.

Um, I don't think so, Dr. Hartley.

I couldn't imagine anything more embarrassing than a public weigh-in. Except maybe that time at the beach when I got back from boogie boarding and Jason Kemp, who is the cutest guy I have ever met and has beautiful tan eyes that perfectly match his beautiful tan body, pointed out that I had a long, green, slimy thingie hanging from my nose. That was definitely way up there on my most-embarrassing list, but I was suffering from a nasty cold and sinus infection at the time, so in my opinion, the long, green thingie wasn't totally my fault.

Dr. Hartley reached for my elbow and gently guided me toward the scale. No, this wasn't going to happen. I dug my fluorescent-yellow flip-flops into his carpet and stood my ground.

"You know what, Dr. Hartley? My foot just fell asleep, and if I stand on the scale I might fall over on my face and slice open my chin and have to get stitches, and it would be a real shame to start school with stitches on my face, don't you think?"

Dr. Hartley laughed.

"You're a hoot, Sammie. You've been making me laugh since you were a toddler. You're a real character, young lady."

Good. Keep laughing. The more you laugh, the less you'll think about weighing me.

"Come on," Dr. Hartley said, refusing to be deterred. "Height and weight. It just takes a second."

Yeah, a second for the weigh-in, but forever to get over the embarrassment.

Charlie had already gotten weighed and measured. She was five feet two and, of course, a perfect 105 pounds. I knew I was the same height because we're identical twins, and we'd been exactly the same height from the day we were born. But as my family likes to point out, when she was born she weighed a delicate five pounds two ounces, and I came busting out weighing in at a hefty six pounds twelve ounces. That's not big for a regular baby, but for a twin, it's pretty chubby. The family joke has always been that when we were in our mom's belly, I hogged all the food. That used to be funny, but over the last couple of years, as my weight has seriously zoomed ahead of Charlie's, I'm not finding the hog jokes so funny anymore.

In fact, not at all funny.

I'm not what you would call fat. But I'm not what you would call slim, either. Standing there in Dr. Hartley's office, I was positive I weighed at least fifteen pounds more than Charlie, and I wasn't exactly dying to share that news with the whole group. Especially my dad. I would have sooner told the random plumber what I weigh than tell my dad. He's our tennis coach, and when he isn't talking about serves and volleys and topspin and mental toughness, he's lecturing us about weight. I'm sick of it, and so is Charlie, especially since she doesn't even have a weight problem.

"If you want to be champions, you have to be quick on your feet," Dad tells us at least once a week. "And you can't move your feet if you're dragging a big butt around behind you," he adds with a special glance in my direction.

Funny, I'm not aware of dragging my butt around behind me. It just seems to follow me wherever I go, which I've grown used to. I mean, what else would be behind me if not my butt?

"Sammie, did you hear Dr. Hartley?" I heard my

dad say. "He wants you on the scale." He sounded irritated, but that was no surprise. He's not big on patience, my dad.

"Actually, Dad, I didn't hear him. Maybe instead of checking my weight, we should check my hearing."

"Yeah," Ryan piped up. "We don't want her to be fat *and* deaf."

Thank you, big brother Ryan. Always there when a girl needs a little love.

"Ryan, why don't you go back in the bathroom where you belong?" Charlie snapped, coming to my rescue. "We'll call you when we want your opinion. Which, by the way, is never."

"Up you go, Sammie," said Dr. Hartley. "Let's see what Mr. Scale has to tell us."

Maybe that "Mr. Scale" stuff is amusing to four-year-olds with leg rashes, but I am twelve and three quarters, and it wasn't amusing to me. Personally, I hoped Mr. Scale would blow up and die.

I was out of excuses. I stepped on the scale and closed my eyes. I could hear Dr. Hartley pushing that little metal weight—which had been set on 105 pounds for Charlie—up and up and up.

No more up, please. Make it stop. Make it stop.

"One two six and a half," he said, after it seemed like he had been fiddling with that stupid weight forever.

I'm no math genius, but I knew that "one two six and a half" was a nice way of saying that I weighed one hundred and twenty-six and a half pounds. You don't want to leave out the half.

"Someone's going to have to cut out the ice cream and candy bars," my dad blurted out. "Right, Sammie?"

I wanted to cry and yell at the same time. There should be a word for that, like *crell*. Yeah, that's it: I wanted to crell. I wanted to tell him that I don't sit around stuffing my face with ice cream and candy bars, that I eat a ton of salad, and that if I ate another bag of those baby carrots I was going to turn orange and get eaten by a rabbit.

"Dad," Charlie whispered. "Not a good topic. Not now."

"Don't be silly, Charlie," my dad said. "Now is always the best time to deal with things. Besides, we're all family here."

Really? I didn't know that I was related to the whining four-year-old with the leg rash or that the random plumber was my long-lost uncle Fred.

"There's nothing to be ashamed of, Sammie," Dr. Hartley said. "You just have to make some better food choices and continue to get lots of exercise."

"Yeah," my dad agreed. "Then you'll weigh what Charlie weighs. Lean muscle, quick feet, no extra drag—that's what we're going for."

"Rick," Dr. Hartley said, holding up his hand to stop my dad from going on. "Sammie's a bright girl. She gets the point."

I hate being compared to Charlie. We're different.

Sure, she weighs less and probably always will. But I can whistle and she can't. And her third toe on her right foot is longer than her second toe and mine isn't. And I have a pink birthmark on my upper arm that looks like a baby ladybug, and she doesn't have any birthmarks at all. The point being that even though Charlie and I are identical twins, we're not identical. We're *almost* identical. My dad just doesn't get that.

Thank goodness Dr. Hartley took Charlie and me into a private examining room for the rest of the checkup. He listened to our hearts and checked that our spines were straight. He talked to us about using good judgment now that we were going into seventh grade and not giving in to peer pressure. When it came to diet and weight, he said that I was at the high end of normal and reminded me that I should focus on eating lots of healthy fruits and vegetables. If I wanted, he had a nutritionist I could see. And then he dropped the subject, which was a giant relief. Another giant relief was that we didn't have to get any shots this year. I'm not a fan of sharp needles.

When we left Dr. Hartley's office, I was so relieved to see GoGo waiting for us in the lobby. She's our grandmother. Our mom's mom. She's taking care of us for a year because our mom has gone across the country to Boston to study cooking so she can come back to Los Angeles and open a restaurant. I miss my mom a lot, but GoGo makes it bearable because she's so much fun. Charlie and I named her GoGo when we were little because she's always on the go with, like, a thousand fun things a minute. She takes us to the beach and to the mall and to art classes at the museum and to movies and to a bead store where you can make your own bracelets. Everything she does is fun.

"Who's up for ice cream?" she asked. It was one of our traditions. Whenever we went to the doctor to get a shot or a strep throat test or a checkup, GoGo would magically appear in the lobby and take us for ice cream afterward.

"I'm in," Ryan said.

"Root-beer float for me," Charlie agreed.

"What are you craving, Sammie?" GoGo asked, throwing her tan arm around my shoulder. I heard her silver bracelets jangling next to my ear, but I didn't look up. I could feel my dad staring at me.

"I'm not in the mood for ice cream," I said, which was a total lie, because I was seriously dying for a scoop of cappuccino chocolate chip with hot caramel sauce and two cherries on the side. I had been thinking about it all morning.

GoGo gave me a funny look. She knew something was up.

"Sammie nearly broke the scale in the doctor's office," Ryan told her. "We're sewing her mouth shut."

"Nonsense," GoGo answered. "Sammie has a healthy, robust body."

"Oh yeah? Then how come she weighs a ton?"

GoGo shot Ryan a stern look. "Bodies come in all shapes and sizes. Sammie is a healthy young woman, and that's what matters."

I wanted to drop into the floor and disappear. Since when was my body a topic of conversation?

Hey, everyone join in. Oh you, Mr. Police Officer on the corner giving a parking ticket, what do you think of my body? Step right up and comment.

"I don't want to discuss it anymore, okay?" I snapped. And by the tone of my voice, everyone knew I was about two seconds away from crying. Even Ryan just shrugged and shut up.

So we went to the ice-cream place and everyone else ordered. Me? I had nothing. Not a lick, not a sip, not a swallow.

The only things I swallowed were my tears.

The
Sporty Forty

....

Chapter 2

"Wake up, Sammie! Now! Emergency!"

I could feel Ryan shaking my shoulder hard, trying to wake me from a really deep sleep. I had been dreaming I was a baby elephant climbing a palm tree to get a coconut. It was a frustrating dream, because I think we all know that baby elephants are not good tree climbers. Actually, neither are grown-up elephants, but that's besides the point.

"What's the emergency?" I muttered, rolling over in bed.

"Only, like, the biggest tornado *ever!*" Ryan shouted. "It's moving down the coast, coming right for us."

Did he say *tornado*? In Southern California? I had never heard of a tornado hitting Los Angeles before.

Ryan sounded really scared. "Move fast, Sam. We have to evacuate! Dad is packing everything up."

I jumped out of bed and ran to the window, my heart beating fast. We live right on the beach in Santa Monica. I mean, *right* on the beach: Our house sits smack on the sand, about fifty feet from the Pacific Ocean. I wanted to scan the beach for a kayak so maybe I could row out to sea to get out of the tornado's path.

"Sammie, get away from the window!" Ryan warned. "We've got to bail *right now.*"

I had to see what was going on. I threw back the curtain, blinded at first by the bright morning light that was streaming in. I looked out at our beach and as my eyes adjusted to the sunlight, I saw . . .

NOTHING! No high winds. No tornado twisting its way to us. No pounding surf. Just the calm ocean, the sparkling sand, and the red-cushioned, wooden beach lounge chairs of our beach club waiting for someone to lie on them.

I looked over at Ryan, and he was laughing like the idiot boy he is.

"Not funny, dude," I said to him.

"Oh, that's where you're wrong, little sister," he howled. "Very funny. Extremely funny. Seriously hilarious, in fact. You should have seen your face!"

I confess: I do not understand the boy sense of humor. They burp, then they laugh. They expel gas, then they laugh. They see a girl's flip-flop get stuck on a big wad of bubblegum, then they laugh. (I know, because that happened to me a couple months ago at the mall and Ryan and his club volleyball team buddies couldn't stop yukking it up.)

Real grown-up.

"You have a very twisted sense of humor," I said to Ryan. My heart was just beginning to slow down.

"Well, I had to do something radical to get you out of bed," he told me. "Dad said he wants you out on the tennis court in five minutes. He's been hitting with Charlie for a half hour already."

We have two tennis courts about a twenty-second walk from my bedroom. I know that sounds like we're rich, but we're totally not. My dad works at this private beach and tennis club called the Sporty Forty, and as part of his pay we get to live in the bungalow that was built for the caretaker. So that makes us the opposite of rich.

I reached for my cell phone to check the time. It was ten fifteen. Oops—I was supposed to meet Dad on the court at ten. My mom always used to make sure that I was up on time since I have a serious tendency to oversleep. But for the last two weeks, since Mom left for cooking school, I have been sleeping through everything. Maybe I shouldn't have stayed up half the night decorating my scrapbook with those furry tennis ball stickers GoGo bought me. I love to stay up at night to do projects and then sleep late the next day. Charlie, on the other hand, is asleep by ten o'clock and wakes up early, all bright and ready to go.

Ryan was still hanging around our room, poking his nose into my scrapbook.

"I don't think you have enough of those cute, furry stickers in here," he said. "Look, you missed an inch."

"For your information, they are not just cute, they also serve a purpose. I put one next to each picture of when Charlie and I won a match."

"Oh, I get it. You're matching them with your matches." Then, realizing what he had said, he burst out laughing. "A match match, get it? Man, I crack myself up."

"Apparently it doesn't take much."

"Come on, Sam. You have to admit that's funny. Or at least *punny.*" Unbelievable as it seems, he laughed again at that not-even-a-little-bit-funny remark.

"You and your ace sense of humor can leave now," I told Ryan. "I have to get dressed. And by the way, thanks for scaring me to death."

"No problem, Sam-I-Am. Any time." Ryan flashed me a smile and then—you're not going to believe this— he winked at me. You heard me. My *brother* winked at me. Obviously, he was trying to work out some cool, new move that he could use on the girls at school, but I'm sorry, it is unacceptable to try it out on me. Totally unacceptable.

"I think you have something in your eye," I said. "It looks really painful."

Then he winked *again* as if it weren't bad enough the first time. I had no choice but to throw

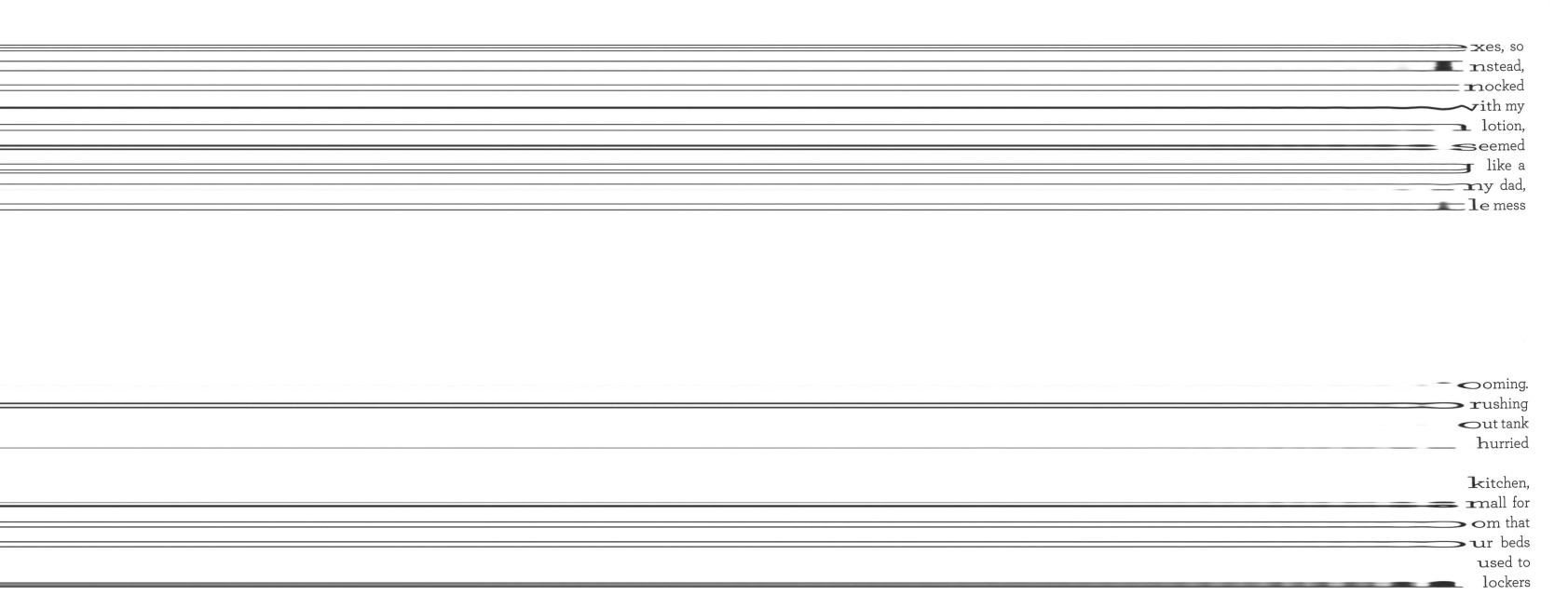

xes, so
nstead,
nocked
with my
lotion,
seemed
like a
my dad,
le mess

ooming.
rushing
out tank
hurried

kitchen,
mall for
om that
ur beds
used to
lockers

all along one wa

the living room,

up with him in it

Our old hou

but we had to s

year. While we

dad's college bu

be the athletic d

Forty. They call

owned by the sa

They're all prett

tennis like my

until he messed

When Chip sai

cottage for free,

could save a lot

school, and whe

a restaurant tog

house again."

So one mont

bungalow of the

mom left for Bos

Even though

all the time, livi

sweet arrangeme

waves breaking fr

to the beach all

too. It has two t

practice whenev

And there's constant beach volleyball for Ryan, who, besides being an idiot boy, is a major volleyball champion and all-around jock.

GoGo was in the kitchen when I came running in. She helps out at the club when there are parties and stuff, so I figured there must be a party that day. GoGo used to have a little shop near the Venice boardwalk called Moonstone, where she sold beautiful silver jewelry she made by hand. But business hadn't been great lately, so she closed her shop and sells at craft fairs instead. When we moved into the Sporty Forty, Chip Wadsworth asked her if she'd have time to help organize their events, and she said sure. She loves parties, and besides, working there gives her extra money and plenty of time to make her jewelry and take care of us, too.

"Morning, Sammie," she said. "I put some sliced cantaloupe for you on the counter."

"Thanks, GoGo, but I'm late."

"It's never too late for fruit."

She held the plate out for me with a look that said *You will eat this cantaloupe and enjoy it.* I grabbed a slice and stuffed it in my mouth, reaching down to tie my shoes at the same time. I must not have totally closed my lips because as soon as I bit down, some juice shot out of my mouth onto my shoe.

"Oh, great," I groaned. "Now my shoes are all cantaloupey."

GoGo laughed and handed me a napkin.

"When will you learn? You're always late, always rushing. That makes life messy."

"Squirty cantaloupe makes life messy."

"You should have gotten up on time, Doodle. Noodle has been on the court with your father for a half hour already."

In case you're wondering why GoGo was speaking in rhyme, Doodle and Noodle are her special nicknames for us. My real name is Samantha Ellen Diamond, mostly known as Sammie, except that GoGo calls me Doodle. My sister is Charlotte Joy Diamond, mostly known as Charlie, but in GoGo-speak, she's Noodle or, sometimes, The Noodle. I'm not sure how I got to be Doodle and she got to be Noodle, but I'm guessing it's because she was always thin like a noodle and I was round like a doodlebug.

Oh, there it is again. The weight thing. Why is it always on my mind even when it's not on my mind?

GoGo reached up to the shelves above the sink, pulled out a whole bunch of platters and trays, and started to wipe them off.

"I think the brownies will look really nice on this silver one," she said, holding up a beautiful, shiny tray.

"Brownies? Yum. I love brownies!"

Oh, I forgot. No, Sammie. No brownies for you. Not at one two six and a half.

"Is there a party tonight?" I asked, stuffing another cantaloupe slice into my mouth to drive out the thought of those evil, chocolaty brownies.

"It's Lauren Wadsworth's thirteenth birthday party," GoGo said. "She's having about thirty people. Lots of kids from your new school will be there. I'm sure Lauren won't mind if you and Charlie go."

Grown-ups always think that just because you're the same age as another kid, you'll want to hang out with them and they'll want to hang out with you. What even a cool grown-up like GoGo didn't understand was that Lauren Wadsworth was the most perfect, most popular, most *everything* girl at Beachside Middle School. Charlie and I hadn't even started school there yet, but we already knew about her. Even at Culver, our old middle school, she was famous for being rich, smart, beautiful, and everything else you'd ever want to be.

"We can't go to her party, GoGo. We don't even know Lauren Wadsworth."

"I hear she's a darling girl. And you are darling girls. So it's a perfect fit."

Yeah, right, a perfect fit. Charlie and I had seen Lauren a few times at the club over the last month, and she didn't exactly come over and ask to be our new best friend. She just hung out with her group, the other girls from the club, like Brooke Addison, Jillian Kendall, and Lily March. None of those girls seemed like they were dying to get to know the two new, girl, jock tennis players who were living in the caretaker's bungalow and transferring in from Culver City Middle School.

I grabbed my racket and headed outside. It was another perfect day: the sun shining, the red beach umbrellas of the club fluttering in the ocean breeze. On the first court, four members were playing doubles—older women with floppy hats and even floppier upper arms. On the second court, Charlie was practicing her serve, and Dad was calling out instructions.

"Toss the ball higher, Charlie. Raise your point of contact. Don't overpower it—go for accuracy!"

When Charlie saw me, she stopped serving and came running over. She gave me a hug, her hot cheek pressing against my cool one. I immediately felt guilty that she was out there working so hard and I was the slacker, as usual.

"Is he mad that I'm late?" I whispered.

"I told him you had to put new shoelaces in."

"How'd you come up with that?"

"I don't know. Sometimes I amaze myself." Charlie giggled.

I love my sister. She's always there for me when I screw up. Of course, I'm there for her, too, but she doesn't screw up nearly as often as I do, that's for sure.

"Get your game face on," she whispered as Dad came jogging up to us. "He's very hyped-up about the tournament."

"How're the new shoelaces?" my dad asked, wiping the sweat from his forehead with his wristband.

"So much better, Dad. Those old ones were . . ." I hesitated and looked over at Charlie, not knowing what she had told him.

"Really ratty," she chimed in, moving her body in front of mine so my shoelaces weren't visible.

"And full of cantaloupe juice," I added for an authentic touch.

"Glad you changed them," he said. "You want to look your best for the tournament tomorrow. You do remember you girls are playing in a tournament tomorrow, don't you, Sammie?"

"Course I do, Dad."

How could I forget? The 12th Annual Sand and Surf Club Satellite Classic was the next day, and our dad had been talking about it nonstop for two weeks. It was a really important tournament, because if we won both of our matches, we'd get enough total points to qualify for a state ranking. And that was really, really important to Dad.

Charlie and I had been ranked twenty-second in the state in the Under-12 Girls Doubles category. Not to brag or anything, but that's pretty good. I mean, California is a big state with a lot of very competitive tennis players. But after we turned twelve, we had to move up to an older category, the Under-14, and we were still trying to accumulate enough points to get our ranking back. You get so many points for each match you win, and when you get enough, you get a ranking.

Our dad is totally focused on our getting a ranking. He has it all planned out for us kids: Ryan is going to go to college on a volleyball scholarship, and Charlie and I are going to get tennis scholarships. At least that's what he thinks. In our family, the purpose of sports isn't to have fun and get exercise. It's to win, to be the best. Our future, our education, everything depends on it.

I know what you're thinking. "No pressure there!" Yeah, tell me about it.

"I'll warm up Sammie," my dad said to Charlie, "while you go hydrate."

Hydrate is sports-guy talk for *get a drink of water.* I've learned that if you play sports seriously, you have to use the right vocab. I mean, if you say "I'm thirsty," it just sounds like your mouth is dry. But if you say "I need some hydration," well, that sounds like you're ready to compete in the Olympics.

Charlie went in the kitchen, and my dad started hitting with me, yelling at me to move my feet, to lunge for the ball, to quicken my reaction time. He was right, of course, but what did he want from me? I mean, like five minutes before I had been sound asleep. You don't just wake up and start lunging for the ball. At least *I* don't.

When Charlie came back from "hydrating," Ryan was tagging along behind her. He had tied a red bandanna around his head like he was the Karate Kid or something. It covered his forehead and held his long, blond hair back from his face. On anyone else, that bandanna would have looked totally stupid. But

Ryan has a way of taking the oddest things and making them look cool. Don't get me wrong: I don't think he's cool at all, but I happen to know that lots of other people do. All of our friends at our old school always acted really flirty when he was around and constantly told us how cute he was. They wouldn't have thought that if they knew he puts green beans in his nose and makes monkey noises at the dinner table.

"There's Ry Guy," my dad said when he saw Ryan. "Tell you what, handsome: Let's you and me play a doubles set against Sammie and Charlie. What do you say, girls? Can you whip us?"

"*Them* whip *us*?" Ryan laughed. "No way!"

"Oh, yes way," Charlie shot back.

"We'll eat you alive," I added. "I have a certain tornado story I need to get even for."

"I still can't believe you bit on that one."

Ryan was laughing about it all over again, which made me even more determined to whip his butt on the tennis court. I know it sounds impossible for Charlie and me to beat one almost-professional grown-up man and his total jock of a son, but it wasn't out of the question. Charlie and I are very competitive. She's light on her feet and quick at the net. I move slower, but I have a lot of power at the baseline. Each of us makes up for what the other doesn't have. Dad says we are like two halves of a circle, born to play doubles tennis.

We started the set, and Charlie and I were playing

great. We were tied at three games each, and I was beginning to think we had a chance. But then we had to quit because Mr. Hornblower arrived for his eleven o'clock tennis lesson with Dad. Ryan wanted to play a tiebreaker, but Mr. Hornblower didn't want to wait. He's a total grump, although I have to say, I would be, too, if my name were Mr. Hornblower.

Dad started his lesson, and Charlie and I headed into the kitchen. I really needed to hydrate because I was sweating like a pig. Charlie always manages to look good when she sweats. She just gets a moist glow all over her face. Me? I get these big globs of sweat that pop out on my upper lip, and no matter how many times I wipe them off, they just seem to bubble back out again. And my hair, which is normally dark blond, gets wet and stringy and turns the color of baby poop. I think we can all agree that's not an attractive look.

So you can imagine how I felt when my baby-poop hair and I walked into the kitchen to find Lauren Wadsworth sitting at the counter with GoGo. She was wearing a sundress with swirly, yellow flowers and sandals with yellow jewels to match. Her hair, which is very shiny and the color of maple syrup, was held back in a yellow headband that totally matched her dress. She looked like she had just stepped out of a suntan lotion ad in *Seventeen* magazine. She and GoGo were in a deep discussion about whether the brownies should go on the silver tray or the blue tray with pink seashells.

"Hi, kids," GoGo said. "You all know Lauren, don't you?"

Lauren turned and gave us a really nice smile. I could smell her lip gloss—it was strawberry. She must have just put it on. I glanced at my reflection in the glass panes of the cupboard. Yup, those big globs of sweat were definitely there on my upper lip. I wiped them off with my arm, but I swear they squirted out again before I had even said hello to Lauren.

"Happy birthday," Charlie said to her.

"Thanks." Lauren looked at her jelly watch that had the cutest fluorescent-orange band you've ever seen. "I'll be thirteen in three hours and twelve minutes."

"Then you'll officially be a teenager," I added, tucking my sticky, loose hair back into my ratty ponytail. It was hopeless—why didn't I just give up? I'm sure Lauren was thinking that I was the most disgusting creature she had ever seen.

But then I noticed that Lauren wasn't looking at my hair—or at me at all. She wasn't looking at Charlie, either. She was smiling at someone behind us, someone wearing a red bandanna and grinning right back at her.

"Hi, Ryan," she said, her teeth looking very white against her strawberry lip gloss.

"Hey, Lauren. Nice tan."

The two of them just stood there smiling at each other like goons. GoGo didn't seem to notice that a major flirt-fest was going on. Or if she did, she didn't let on.

"We're making all kinds of critical decisions for Lauren's party tonight," she said, holding up the silver tray and the blue one with pink seashells. "Which one should we put the brownies on?"

"I'd go with the seashell one," Ryan said. "We're at the beach and all."

Lauren nodded enthusiastically.

"Great thought, Ryan."

Really? What's so great about it? Look around: There's the sand. There's the ocean. There's the beach. How hard is that to figure out?

"Sounds like you're going to have a fun party," Ryan said to her.

"Why don't you come, Ryan? All my friends are going to be there."

GoGo put the trays down and looked up, a big smile on her face.

"Oh, what a lovely invitation, Lauren. I'm sure the girls would be happy to join, too. Wouldn't you, girls?"

GoGo! Are you kidding me???? She didn't invite us; she invited Ryan. Did you not notice?

Lauren looked a little surprised, but GoGo put her tan arm around Lauren's shoulder and gave her a really big smile.

"It will be such a nice opportunity for Charlie and Sammie to meet some kids from Beachside."

"Yeah, I guess," Lauren said. What else could she say? "Oh, I didn't mean to invite *them,* I only wanted *him*"? No, only a total jerk would say that, and actually, she didn't seem like a jerk at all—she seemed really friendly.

"It's at six o'clock," Lauren said. "Here on the beach."

"Cool," Charlie said. "We'll see you later. What should we wear?"

"Shorts. Jeans. It's totally whatever."

"You'd better get a move on, Sam," Ryan said. "If you're going to be out in public, you've got some serious work to do on that hair."

Lauren giggled like he had just said the funniest thing ever. It's amazing what a guy can get away with when he looks good in a bandanna. I was about to open my mouth and let him know what I thought of his tennis-shoes-with-no-socks look, but Charlie grabbed my hand and pulled me out of the kitchen before I could say anything.

"Not now," she whispered as she yanked me into our room.

"Why? He deserves it after that hair remark."

"Because Lauren likes him and we want to make a good impression on her."

"We do? Why?"

"Because she's Lauren Wadsworth."

"So?"

"So we're the new kids and she's really popular, and it would make everything so much easier at school if we could be friends with her."

"But we don't even know if we like her yet."

"It doesn't matter, Sammie."

"I see."

"Of course you do. We're twins. We agree on everything, right?"

I nodded, but deep down I wasn't nodding. I actually didn't agree with what Charlie was thinking. I wasn't sure I wanted to be friends with Lauren Wadsworth, and even more important, I wasn't sure she wanted to be friends with me.

The Party

....

Chapter 3

"Please tell me you're not seriously wearing that," Charlie said as I came out of our room.

We had spent all afternoon discussing what to wear to Lauren's party. After trying on everything she owns, Charlie decided to keep it simple: white shorts and a pink tee with a peace sign in purple rhinestones. I was clearly going to wear jeans instead of shorts. Finding out that you officially weigh one two six and a half doesn't exactly make you feel confident enough to show off your thigh region to a bunch of kids you've never met before.

At first I put on a red knit top, but after staring at myself in the mirror for at least twenty minutes, I concluded that it showed too much boob. I'm still not entirely used to the fact that I have boobs at all, so I for sure didn't want to flaunt them. I figured that since I was meeting all new kids, I didn't need to introduce my boobs to everyone before anyone even knew my name.

So off went the red top and on went a black-and-white striped top. I checked out that look in the mirror and decided that black-and-white horizontal stripes made me look like an overweight zebra. Definitely not the look I was going for.

Finally I put on a loose T-shirt that I bought earlier in the summer when we took the backlot tour at Universal Studios as a going-away celebration for Mom. It's your basic black tee, except across the front it says *I Do All My Own Stunts*. I was so amazed at the Universal Studios stunt show, at how all those cowboys threw themselves off the tops of buildings and those race car drivers slammed into walls of flaming fires, that I just had to buy a souvenir. It's like after we took this amazing hike down into the Grand Canyon, I got a T-shirt that said *Mules are for Sissies*. I thought of that hike every time I wore it.

"What's wrong with this shirt?" I asked Charlie. "I think it's cool."

"It's just so weird, Sammie. Why would you wear a *souvenir* to a party?"

"It's a good conversation starter. I bet everyone who sees me will ask what stunts I do, and then I can say something clever."

"Such as?"

Oops—I hadn't thought that far ahead. It was definitely not good to wear a conversation starter that you couldn't converse about.

"I'll come up with something at the appropriate time," I reassured her. "Don't you worry. You look great, by the way."

Charlie adjusted the purple headband in her hair. With her hair pulled away from her face, you could really see the freckle just over her left eyebrow. I have the exact same one, but mine is over my right eyebrow. Even though they're just plain, old, regular freckles, GoGo calls them our beauty marks. She has a way of making you feel good about everything.

"Okay," I said, taking Charlie's hand and starting down the wooden path to the beach. "I guess it's time to make our entrance."

"Sammie, are you nervous?"

"Why should I be nervous? Just because we're meeting *all* new kids who *all* know one another and are *all* going to think we're weird for crashing their party? Of course I'm nervous."

"Good."

I stopped in my tracks and gave her a look.

"That sounded horrible," Charlie apologized. "I didn't mean it's good that you're nervous, but good that we're both nervous so I don't feel so bad about being the only one who is really nervous. You know what I mean?"

"The question is, do *you* know what you mean?"

"I don't have a clue," she said, and we both laughed. A nervous laugh.

As we passed outside the kitchen, I could see GoGo through the window arranging vegetables around a big bowl of ranch dip. She loves to arrange food, and since she's so artistic, she makes everything into a beautiful design. I could see her standing up the broccoli like little trees and arranging rings of red pepper into a necklace surrounding the dip.

"You look adorable, girls," she called out as she saw us walk by. "Have fun!"

Easier said than done when you're crashing a party and don't know a soul.

The tennis courts are on one side of the wooden beach path and the Sporty Forty members' deck area is on the other. It faces the wide Santa Monica beach and usually has chaise lounges and umbrellas set up for the members to lie around and sunbathe and talk on their cell phones. But all the furniture had been cleared away to make a dance floor for the party. A deejay was playing an old Beyoncé song and a few kids were dancing. At the far end of the dance floor was a huge banner that said *Happy Birthday, Lauren!*

Out on the beach, a few boys were tossing around a Frisbee, and my dad was there lighting tiki torches. Or at least *trying* to light tiki torches. He was having a tough time because the wind kept blowing them out, and I could tell by the way he hunched his shoulders that he was annoyed. No surprise there. He's the king of being annoyed. But everyone else seemed to be having a great time laughing and talking and hanging out.

Charlie and I walked up to the edge of the dance floor and stopped.

"Now what?" I whispered to her.

"Now two really cute guys come up and ask us to dance. That's the way it happens in the movies."

Charlie looked around and put her best smile out there for anyone who was interested. No one was. Not only did no one ask us to dance, no one even came up to say hi.

"Wow, this is awkward," I said. "Let's go back inside."

I was seriously considering running back to our room when a familiar voice called out from the far end of the dance floor.

"Come on out here, Charlie. Yo, Sammie, show everyone your moves."

It was Ryan. He was dancing with Lauren, smiling and laughing like all her friends were already his best friends.

"Let's show them how we Diamonds do it," he

called, and then went into his robot dance routine that he practices nonstop in front of the mirror.

A bunch of kids turned to see if we were going to join Ryan.

Not me. I would rather die. Maybe *that* Diamond doesn't mind making a spectacle of himself, but *this* one does!

Ryan went through his robot routine, then he dropped to the floor and launched into a scissors kick and backspin. My brother has about six dance steps, or as he calls them, "power moves." They're all pretty bad, but the amazing thing is, he pulls them off. He's just got this confident attitude that what he's doing is cool, and before you know it, it is! Obviously, I didn't inherit that quality.

"Do you want to dance?" someone asked from behind us. I whirled around to see a cute, redheaded guy smiling and holding out his hand. I was just about to answer when I realized that he wasn't asking *me* to dance, he was asking *Charlie*.

"Do you mind?" she whispered to me.

"Go ahead. I'll be fine."

The truth is, I wasn't fine. As I watched Charlie follow him out onto the deck, I felt like a total nerd standing there by myself. I stared down at my feet, and when I looked up, what I saw was everyone else dancing. I tried to pretend I was having a great time and plastered a frozen, fake smile on my face. When I couldn't hold that smile a second longer, I turned and bolted out to the beach where some boys had organized a game of Frisbee football. Maybe joining in a Frisbee game was the best way for me to break the ice.

"Anyone want to toss me one?" I asked.

"This is a serious game," a boy in plaid shorts and glasses said. "Notice how you don't see other girls out here."

"Maybe they can't catch," I shot back, trying to sound more confident than I felt. "Try me. I'm going long."

The boy in the plaid shorts looked at the other guys and shrugged. I took off running down the beach, and he tossed a long throw in my direction. It was over my head, so I sprinted as hard as I could and had to jump high off the sand to just barely catch the Frisbee by the rim. But I caught it.

"Nice grab," the boy with the glasses hollered. "Is that one of your stunts?"

Okay, Sammie. Time to say something clever about the T-shirt. Here's the moment you were waiting for.

"Sure is," I called out. It was all I could come up with and not exactly a brilliant conversation starter. But at least someone answered.

"Where'd you learn to catch like that?" one of the guys asked.

"My brother, Ryan. I've played catch with him since I could walk."

I tossed the Frisbee back to one of the guys—with

dead-on aim, I might add—and jogged back to join their group.

"Oh, so you're Ryan's sister. He's a great dude."

"Fun guy," another one agreed.

"I'm Sammie Diamond," I said. "Short for Samantha."

They went around the circle and each guy introduced himself. There was Ben in the plaid shorts and glasses, Jared in the long basketball shorts, Spencer in the jeans and white T-shirt, and the General in the camouflage pants. I'm pretty sure that wasn't his real name, but I said, "Nice to meet you, General," anyway. And then I saluted.

"At ease, soldier," he said, and we all laughed.

This is a good beginning, Sammie. Everyone's laughing. Laughing is good.

As the laughter died out, there was an awkward silence. They didn't seem to be inviting me into their game, so I thought maybe they wanted to just talk instead.

"My sister, Charlie, and I are starting Beachside on Monday," I began. "Seventh grade."

"You're both in seventh grade?" Spencer asked. "How does that work?"

"Yeah, did one of you get left behind?" the General said, and everyone laughed.

"No, we're twins. She's over there dancing."

The kid named Jared looked over at Charlie, who was still dancing with the redheaded guy.

"Yeah, I see her. She's the hot version of you."

Ouch. That hurts. Why do boys always say things that hurt?

I tried to make a joke of it. What else was I going to do? Cry?

"She's from the hot side of the family. I got the mac 'n' cheese gene."

I gave an awkward, little laugh, but no one else did.

"Sucks to be you," Jared said.

Then they all laughed again. Honestly, it wasn't even funny. It was just mean. I couldn't laugh along with them. I just wanted to run away and hide. So without even a good-bye, I turned and ran down the beach toward the water, far enough away from them so they couldn't see my face and I couldn't see theirs. When I reached the last of the tiki torches that my dad had finally gotten lit, I flopped down in the sand and took a deep breath, trying to hold back my tears.

"I hate them," I muttered to myself. "I truly hate them."

"They're just being guys," said a voice.

I nearly jumped out of my skin. I had thought I was totally alone there on the sand, in a quiet spot except for the sound of the waves lapping the shore. But when I whipped around, I noticed a girl standing in the shadow of the tiki torch. She was really pretty, with shiny, black hair that reflected the flickering flames from the torch. I was so embarrassed that she heard what I said. She was probably best friends with all these kids, and here I was being Miss Negative.

"I didn't mean hate them as in *real* hate," I said. "Just *kind of* hate, like the temporary kind."

"I get it," she said with a smile. "That's cool."

Wow, could this actually be someone being nice to me? That was a welcome change.

I noticed she was wearing a beautiful white top with orange and blue flowers embroidered all across the front.

"That's a great shirt," I said.

"Thanks. It's from El Salvador, where I'm from."

"Oh. When did you come here? I mean, your English is really great."

"I was born there, but my parents came to California when I was three. I've been speaking English for a long time."

I nodded. She was really friendly.

"My name is Alicia, by the way. Alicia Bermudez."

"Hey. I'm Sammie Diamond."

"I know," Alicia said. "My parents work with your dad."

"So your parents are . . ."

"Esperanza and Candido. My dad is the groundskeeper here, and my mom comes twice a week to clean."

"Oh, Candido! He's your dad? He always stops by to watch us practice tennis. When he's taking a pineapple break."

"He loves pineapple. I'm surprised he hasn't sprouted leaves on the top of his head."

We both laughed. She had the biggest brown eyes that crinkled up at the sides when she smiled.

"So how do you know my name?" I asked her.

"My father told me about you and your sister. He thinks we should hang out. You know how parents are, always thinking kids should hang out together."

"Tell me about it," I agreed. "That's what I'm doing here. My grandma thinks Charlie and I should hang out with Lauren Wadsworth and her friends. You can see how well that's working out for me."

"But your sister seems happy," Alicia commented, glancing up to the deck where Charlie was now dancing with Ryan. They were both doing the robot, and I have to confess, she looked pretty cute doing it. She's a way better dancer than he is. Ryan couldn't have cared less how he looked, but still, there was a group of girls gathered in a circle around him, anyway, clapping and stuff. Girls just like him. And I'm sure it didn't hurt that he was probably the only eighth-grader there.

"My sister and I are different," I said.

"That's funny, because you look so much alike."

"On the outside. But lots of things are easier for her. Social stuff, especially."

"Yeah, I can see that," Alicia said, but in a really nice way. "If you want, you can hang out with me tonight. I'm going to help my father with the barbecue."

"So you're here to work?"

"Not really. Lauren invited me to the party, but I think mostly because I was here at the club when her mother was telling my parents how to move the furniture and hang the banner. She's not a bad person, and I'm sure she felt sorry for me."

"Felt sorry for you? You're great. Why would anyone feel sorry for you?"

"I'm not really part of their group at school. That's okay, though. I have my own friends who are pretty cool."

"So these kids have an actual group at school?"

Alicia nodded. "They call themselves the SF2s, as in Sporty Forty, second generation. It's not an actual club or anything, but ever since last year when we started middle school, they've gotten pretty tight. They've grown up together, and their parents are all friends."

Our family had moved three times, four including the move to the Sporty Forty. Each time Charlie, Ryan, and I had to make all new friends, and I always envied the kids who had known one another their whole lives. Their relationships were so easy and comfortable. But then, I've always had Charlie, who's not just my sister but also my best friend, so that made the moving not so hard.

Alicia and I stood on the beach and watched the kids dance for a while. She told me about some of them.

"Dan, the redheaded guy, is the star pitcher on

the school baseball team. He's sweet. Brooke Addison, the blonde with the great body—every boy in school is in love with her. She goes out with a guy they call the General."

"I met him," I said. "And saluted."

Alicia laughed again.

"Jillian Kendall, the one with the silver star on her T-shirt, is obsessed with reality TV shows and thinks she's in one. She's always posing."

"Yeah, I've seen her on the beach here. She's very into tanning."

"And Lily March, with the dark, curly hair and the extralong legs—she's already modeled for the Gap catalog."

"Wow," I said. "Are any of the SF2s just regular?"

"Nope."

I watched the kids some more, thinking about what Alicia had told me about each of them. I assumed everyone at school wanted to be them.

Soon the Frisbee guys went up from the beach to join in the dancing, doing some crazy kind of line dance that looked like they had made it up. They moved in unison, and I could tell that they had been doing that same goofy dance together for a long time. They were having fun in the totally comfortable way kids do when they've known one another a long time. Everybody being themselves, nobody having to make a first impression on anyone.

I have to confess, it seemed really fun. And there

were Ryan and Charlie in the middle of it. But Charlie's not the kind of sister who would leave me out. I could see her looking around for me, and when she saw me standing with Alicia out on the beach, she jumped off the deck and ran out to us.

"Sammie," she called. "What are you doing out here?"

"Talking to Alicia. My new friend."

"Hi, new friend. I'm Charlie, her other half. Beautiful shirt."

"Wow," Alicia answered. "You two really do think alike. That was the first thing Sammie said to me, too."

"So what's with you two?" Charlie said, tugging on my arm. "Come on and dance. It's really fun. I'll introduce you to some of the group."

Before I could answer, Charlie grabbed my hand and pulled me toward the deck. I turned around and waved for Alicia to come along, but she shook her head.

"I'm going to help my dad with the burgers," she said. "See you later."

Charlie pushed me out into the center of the dance floor. "This is my sister, Sammie," she said to the kids who were standing around. "She's the best dancer of us all."

I looked over at the group of guys who were on the beach with me, remembering what they said and how bad they'd made me feel. I tried to sway with the music just so I wouldn't stand out, but Ryan wasn't going to let me be inconspicuous.

"Shake that thing, Sam-I-Am," he shouted. Then he went into one of his "power moves" and all the attention turned off me and onto him. When I realized that no one particularly cared if I danced or not, I got into it and didn't feel so self-conscious. I kind of freestyled on my own. After a while, I realized that the music was great, the beach breeze was blowing, the gorgeous moon was coming out, and I was having a good time. While I didn't feel totally at home with these kids, I did like it when Dan, the redheaded pitcher, offered to get me a Sprite.

At one point, I saw GoGo bringing the blue tray of brownies to put on the dessert table. She got the biggest smile ever on her face when she saw Charlie and me dancing and mixing with the other kids. Isn't it amazing how us being even a little bit happy can make our families jump for joy?

When the deejay took a break and it was time for dinner, I looked around for Alicia, but I couldn't find her anywhere. I did see Candido bringing in a platter of burgers from the barbecue.

"Where's Alicia?" I asked him.

"Oh, Alicia, she go home," he said. "I don't understand why, but she say she leaving."

I felt terrible. Maybe he didn't understand why she left, but I did. After all, only an hour before, standing there on the edge of the dance floor with no one talking to me, I had been ready to leave, too. It's the hardest thing in the world, feeling like you don't belong. I wished I had insisted that she come dance with us.

I sat next to Charlie at dinner, and at our table were the boys from the beach: Spencer, Jared, Ben, and the General. Jillian seemed to do a lot of posing for a camera that wasn't there. Charlie was having a good time talking to the boys, but I didn't join in much. I didn't trust them. After all, they had already said that I was the less-hot version of Charlie. How was that supposed to make me feel? Not like carrying on a big old conversation, that's for sure.

Truthfully, the only person I really felt comfortable with the whole night was Alicia, and she had snuck out without anyone even so much as noticing.

No one except me, that is.

The Tournament

....

Chapter 4

"Sammie, stop daydreaming. They're calling your name," my dad said, tapping me on the shoulder to get my attention.

It wasn't so much that I was daydreaming, more that I was just plain tired. It was Sunday at eight in the morning. We were in the courtyard of the Sand and Surf Tennis Club, waiting for the tournament to begin, and I had been up for two hours already. Dragging myself out of bed at six in the morning to warm up before the tournament was a shock to my delicate system. So it was no wonder I didn't notice the loudspeaker calling our names.

"Under-Fourteen Girls," the voice over the loudspeaker blared. "Samantha Diamond and Charlotte Diamond versus Alexis Ha and Michelle

Trippet. All entrants report to court nine."

Charlie handed me my gear and, with our dad talking to us nonstop with last-minute pointers, we headed down the concrete path to our court. GoGo was there, but Ryan wasn't coming until lunchtime. Apparently Ryan had to wait for some friend to arrive, so he was coming in time for our second match.

The Sand and Surf Tennis Club was only a couple miles up Pacific Coast Highway from the Sporty Forty. The Sporty Forty was pretty nice, but this place was a majorly deluxe club, where old-school rich people hung out—the kind of place that had dress codes and social rules. Like no cell phones are allowed around the pool. And you can't wear shorts in the café. I think we can all agree that there is no point whatsoever to being at the beach if you can't wear shorts. For that reason alone, the Sand and Surf Tennis Club has never made any sense to me at all.

But because they had ten tennis courts that were almost brand-new, it's where the Tennis Association held the big satellite tournaments. Charlie and I had recently played in three tournaments there and had done really well. We just had to win two more matches and that would give us enough points to get a state ranking and move up to the divisional circuit. My dad was practically frothing at the mouth to see us get that ranking. Actually, I'm not exactly sure what *frothing* means, but whatever it is, I'm pretty sure he was doing it.

It goes without saying that he wasn't happy with me for daydreaming when I should have been all pumped up for our first match of the 12th Annual Sand and Surf Club Satellite Classic. Even I have to admit, it was a poor time to not be paying attention. My mind is like that, though. It doesn't always cooperate. It has that in common with my hair.

As we headed to court nine, all I could think about was how hot it was. There was no beach breeze and, even at that hour of the morning, the sun beat down on the back of my neck and felt like it was turning my sunscreen into a gooey mess. Our mom had called from Boston that morning to remind us to slather on plenty of sunscreen. She's what you'd call a sunscreen nut. After I promised her I would, I squirted on a huge glob of it, but as I reached up to touch the chemistry experiment that was my neck, I now regretted that I hadn't measured it out more carefully.

Charlie and I were wearing matching outfits, pink, pleated skorts and white tops. We had both pulled our dark-blond hair back in ponytails, and I had put on a visor in the hope of keeping some of my sweat from pouring into my eyes.

Dad couldn't stop talking. He was in his super-duper, intense, motivational coach mode.

"You girls have all the skills you need to win," he said as we reached the gate to the court. "Just keep your heads in the game. Go all out for every shot. Want to win, and you will."

GoGo was walking a little in back of us, carrying a cooler with Gatorade and energy bars. She had on a huge, wide-brimmed straw hat with a leopard-print scarf tied around it. Two women in white tennis outfits and neat, white visors, obviously members of the club, were walking down the path, and I noticed one of them giving GoGo's hat a long stare. GoGo smiled warmly at her.

"That's quite some hat," the woman commented.

"Thank you," GoGo answered. "I like your headgear, too."

"GoGo," I whispered as the women passed by. "I don't think she actually liked your hat."

"Oh, Sammie, in her secret heart, I'll bet she did. You know, girls, everyone longs to be an individual, but most people don't have the courage to stand up and be different."

"Phyllis," my dad said to her, "the girls shouldn't be thinking about hats right now. I want them concentrating on one thing and one thing only. And what is that one thing, girls?"

"Winning," we said in unison.

"Honestly, Rick," GoGo said to Dad. "You make it sound like all the world depends on this match. You put such pressure on these girls."

"Because I believe they can be as great as Serena and Venus Williams. Imagine, two sisters who became the best in the world. And in our case, it would be *twin* sisters. Sammie and Charlie Diamond would rock the whole tennis world."

Notice he said the *whole* tennis world. Not the Los Angeles tennis world. Or the California tennis world. Or even the US tennis world. The *WHOLE* tennis world.

Right, no pressure there.

"The girls want that, too," he added. "Right, Charlie?"

She nodded. She was biting her lower lip like she does when she's really concentrating on her math homework. It's a habit that's part of getting her game face on.

"Agreed, Sammie?" he said, giving me a high five.

I high-fived him back, then tried to concentrate on winning. I really wanted Dad's words to inspire me, but the truth was, I wasn't feeling that confident today. Maybe because it was our first big match since Mom had left for Boston. I didn't have her to calm me down and give me a hug before we went out on the court. Or maybe I was still thinking about that magical number: one two six and a half. Just knowing that I weighed too much made me feel heavier on my feet. As we entered the court, I concentrated on overcoming that feeling.

I have always been a really fierce competitor. Most everyone likes the feeling of winning, but for Charlie and me, it's even more special because we get to share the victory. To look at each other and know that we're a team, that one of us couldn't have done it without the other—it's so great. And the last thing I wanted today was to let her down.

You can do this, Sammie. You are light on your feet. You will fly like the wind. You will win.

My dad gave us a few final words of advice, then he and GoGo went to the stands. Coaches and families aren't allowed on the court during games, only during breaks between sets. That's a good rule, because otherwise, I swear he'd be giving us instructions before, during, and after every shot.

Charlie and I shook hands with the umpire and with the opposing players, Alexis Ha and Michelle Trippet. They had driven up from Orange County, and since we had never played them before, we didn't know what we were up against.

As it turned out, we weren't up against much. They were new to the tournament circuit and didn't give us much of a challenge. In women's tennis, you play the best of three sets. If you each win one set, it's called *split sets,* and you go on to play a third. But if one team wins the first two sets, you don't even have to play a third. And that's what we did. We beat them two sets in a row, and in the second set we were so dominant that the score was six games to love. In tennis, they call zero *love,* which is something I've never understood. It seems to me like *love* should be a million or a trillion, not zero.

"You guys are great," Alexis said when we shook hands after the match.

"I bet you're going to go all the way," her partner,

Michelle, said as the four of us walked off the court together.

"We certainly hope so!" It was my dad, who had leaped from the stands and come down to the sidelines to meet us. He was so excited, you'd think we had just won the US Open. I was embarrassed because Alexis and Michelle weren't really that good—it didn't seem right to be so thrilled about beating them. My dad says I lack the "killer instinct." I suppose I do, but that doesn't seem like such a bad thing to me.

GoGo handed us each a bottle of blue Gatorade and gave bottles to Michelle and Alexis, too.

"You girls did just fine," she told them. "You'll improve with each tournament."

They had been looking pretty dejected, but after GoGo's remark, their faces lit up and they each shook her hand before they walked away to meet their families. Charlie reached over and gave GoGo a hug.

"You're the best," she whispered to her, and I couldn't have agreed more.

Since our next match wasn't scheduled until after lunch, we all went inside the clubhouse to cool off and hydrate. Charlie and I called Mom and told her we'd won, and she screamed so loud, I swear everyone in the club could hear her through the telephone. She said we should call her right after our second match—by that time her cheese soufflé would be out of the oven and she could listen to all the details.

We sat down, and from our chairs by the window we could see onto the center court where the Under-16 Boys were playing singles. I got so involved in watching the match—okay, I confess: so involved in watching the cute guy with the dimples and black Nike headband—that I was surprised when Ryan came up to greet us. I hadn't seen him coming.

Nor had I seen who was walking next to him: It was Lauren Wadsworth.

You're kidding me, Ryan. She's *the friend you're bringing? What happened to your old friends, like weird Winston Chin who can juggle chopsticks? He is way more fun.*

Charlie jumped up and gave Lauren a hug like they had known each other for years. I hadn't realized they had bonded so deeply the night before.

"Lauren, hi!" she said. "Wow, it's great to have you here!"

"I really want to see you guys play," Lauren told us. "Charlie, you look so awesome in that outfit. And Sammie . . . I hear you have a powerful backhand."

Okay, I don't want to be mean here, but let me just point out two things. First, she didn't tell me *I* looked awesome in the outfit, and it was the same outfit Charlie was wearing. And second, I'm willing to bet that until she developed what seemed to be a huge crush on Ryan, Lauren Wadsworth couldn't have cared less about my backhand.

"It's been known to score a point or two," I said.

"My mom sent some lunch for everyone." Lauren put a stack of wrapped sandwiches down on the table. "Tuna, turkey, roast beef. Take your pick."

Before anyone could reach out to make a selection, my dad's hand was in there first.

"This one is best for you," he said, handing me a sandwich. "Turkey. Good, lean protein."

Oh, great. Right in front of Lauren Wadsworth, he's talking about my weight problem. Real sensitive, Dad.

"Turkey is so healthy," Lauren chimed in immediately. "My grandmother is doing Weight Watchers, and that's what she always orders. Turkey, extra mustard, no mayo. She's lost forty pounds. You'd really like her, Sammie."

Wait—did she just say I'd like her grandmother? Why? Because we both weigh a ton? Oh, just kill me now.

I hadn't planned to say anything, but suddenly, my mouth lost control of itself.

"Why would I like her, Lauren? Because we're both overweight? Because we're both stuck eating turkey when everyone else gets to eat whatever they want?"

"Sammie," Charlie said, looking really surprised. "I don't think that's what Lauren meant."

"I think it is," Ryan commented. "She wasn't trying to be mean, dudes. She's just saying it like it is."

Another remark that was so totally not okay.

"Listen, Lauren," I said before I could stop myself. "Nothing against you or anything, but this is a really important tournament, and I think we should just be with our family."

Lauren looked really hurt and embarrassed. She put down her tuna sandwich and started to stand up.

"Oh, I'm sorry. Ryan invited me, and I thought it was okay for me to be here. I'll call my mom to come get me."

She started to walk away, but Charlie reached out and pulled her back.

"Wait, Lauren, I want you to stay." Charlie turned to me. "Sammie, I invited her, too. Lauren wants to see us play, and she's my friend, and I have every right to invite her here."

I was stunned. Charlie hadn't mentioned that she had invited Lauren. She hadn't even asked me if it was okay. That was so weird, because she had had plenty of time to mention it when we were getting ready for bed.

But I really couldn't argue with Charlie. Of course she had the right to ask a friend. And of course I had no business telling her she couldn't. It was just that Lauren made me so uncomfortable. When I was with her, I felt fat and sweaty and . . . well, I don't know, imperfect.

"You're right, Charlie," I said with a sigh. "Of course she can stay."

Everyone went back to eating, and I just stared down at my stupid, dry turkey sandwich. The last thing I wanted to be doing was stuffing in it my face just like old Grandma Wadsworth did. So I excused myself, got up, and headed for the bathroom. When I came out, GoGo was waiting for me at the door. She took me by the elbow and led me outside to the Sand and Surf parking lot that was crammed with Mercedes and BMWs.

"You can talk to me, Doodle," she said. "What's bothering you?"

"I'll be honest, GoGo. I wish Lauren weren't here. She makes me nervous."

"She's being perfectly nice to you, Sammie. She could be a new friend, if you'd let her."

"She doesn't want to be my friend. She wants to be Ryan's girlfriend, and she's just using Charlie and me to get close to him."

"Are you sure about that?" GoGo said. "Because that's a pretty big accusation."

"Why else would she come here and be all nice and bring lunch and everything? She's so different from us."

"Charlie doesn't seem to think so. They're getting along fine."

I tried to think of a good reason for my behavior. I couldn't think of one, but fortunately it didn't matter, because my dad was standing at the entrance to the club, waving.

"Sammie!" he called across the parking lot. "You girls are up! Hustle in here."

I ran across the lot, past an attendant who was washing one of the member's cars. Some of the spray from his hose blew into my face, and it felt great.

"I don't know what was going on out there with you and your grandmother," my dad said when I reached him. "But whatever it was, I hope you left it out there. Tennis is a game of focus. I can't have your mind on other things when you're on the court."

"Don't worry, Dad. I'll get into the game," I said, trying to summon up a little bit of that prized killer instinct.

"That's my girl. Win this one match and you move up to the divisionals. One match. You can do it."

We were assigned to court nine again, and I felt good about that because we had been so lucky there for the first match. As Charlie and I took the court, I glanced up into the stands. It was easy to see where our family was because GoGo's huge hat stuck out from the crowd. My dad sat next to Ryan and Lauren.

Lauren had put on a pink baseball cap, which, of course, looked completely adorable on her. Charlie looked up and waved at Lauren like she was on a desert island and flagging down a passing ship.

"What's with that?" I asked her. "Don't you think it's a little much?"

"It's nice of her to come," Charlie said. "I like her."

"You like *her* or what she represents?"

"Sammie, I don't know what you're talking about."

"The SF2s? Acceptance into their cool group at school?"

"How do you even know their name?"

"Alicia told me. She said they're really tight with one another."

Charlie turned and looked at me. "Look, Sammie. You're my best friend, okay? You'll always be my best friend. But you can't be my *only* friend. I think you're jealous. And I don't think that's very nice."

I had no answer for her, because honestly, I knew what she was saying might be true. Was my bad attitude toward Lauren and her friends just jealousy? Is that why they made me so uncomfortable? Or did I feel that I wasn't good enough to be friends with that group? Either way, my attitude toward Lauren stunk, and I knew it.

All those questions were running around in my mind as we started the match. And I can tell you this right now: They shouldn't have been. These girls we were playing—Caroline Huang and Erin Knight from the Los Angeles Racquet Club—were much better than the last pair. Caroline had the strength of an elephant, and Erin had the speed of a cheetah. I don't know why I suddenly got all jungley on you, but I guess what I'm trying to say is that those girls were all over the court. They didn't miss a shot.

But I did, that's for sure. Not just one shot, but a bunch. We lost the first set, six to three.

Oh, and did I mention we lost the second set, too? In a tiebreaker?

Yup, we did. And guess who served it out of the court three times during the tiebreaker? That's right. Yours truly.

There was no getting around it: I lost the match for us and blew our chances that day to get our ranking.

And if you think I was unhappy about it, you should have heard my dad.

"What happened to you out there?" he said to me after we had shaken hands with our opponents and thanked the umpire. My dad was so steamed up, smoke was practically pouring out of his ears.

"Sorry, Dad. I just wasn't concentrating."

"I could feel it," Charlie put in. "I tried to get you back in the game, but you kept looking up in the stands at Lauren instead of watching the ball."

"I can't help it. I told you, she makes me uncomfortable."

Charlie scowled at me as she took out her hair tie and shook her hair loose. "That's your problem, not hers, Sammie."

"And a pretty weak reason to lose a match," my dad added.

I knew they were right, but I didn't care. Couldn't they understand? I didn't *try* to make us lose. This was something I couldn't control. And now I was being blamed for it. It wasn't fair.

I stomped off the court, over to the chairs where our tennis bags were. I unzipped my bag and pulled out a towel to wipe the giant beads of sweat off my face. I was beet red from the heat, and I was so hot that a little trickle of sweat actually ran down my leg from under my pink, pleated skort. I reached down to wipe it off, and when I looked up, who was watching me but Lauren Wadsworth.

I swear, that girl must have a magic wand that makes her appear every time I couldn't look more gross.

"I'm sorry you lost the match," she said.

Ryan, who was standing next to her, said, "Yeah, what was with you, Sam? You usually play much better."

I could feel a little trickle of sweat running down my leg again.

"Maybe it's the heat," Lauren said as if she could actually console me. "You look really hot."

Thank you, Lauren, for making me even more aware that rivers of sweat are pouring out of inappropriate parts of my body.

"That's our Sammie," Ryan said. "She's a sweater." Then, as he heard what he had said, he cracked up. "Did you hear that? A sweater. She's a bright-red, pullover sweater. I am so *punny*."

Lauren cracked up, too. I had to get away, but there was nowhere to go, so I stuck my face in my towel.

"See you in school tomorrow, Charlie," I heard Lauren say from outside my towel bubble. "I hope we have some classes together."

"Me too," Charlie answered.

"If not, I'll see you at lunch. Meet me at the SF2 table."

As I pulled my face out of the towel, I realized that no one had asked me to lunch. I wasn't invited to the SF2 table; Charlie was.

Oh well, I thought. *Chubby little me probably shouldn't be having lunch, anyway.*

Charlie and I have a tradition where after every competition, win or lose, we go to our favorite pizza place called Barone's and get our favorite pizza, which is sausage and mushroom, and two vanilla Cokes. It's just the two of us, no parents or brother or friends. We call it Pizza Bonding, and we haven't missed one Pizza Bonding since we were ten. So as Lauren and Ryan walked off the court, she turned to me and said, "So how's a sausage and mushroom pizza sound?"

"Fattening."

"We could order a small one."

"Just the two of us?"

"Of course, Sammie. Just the two of us. Like always."

That sounded good to me. It's the way it had always been: just the two of us. But as Lauren reached the gate and waved good-bye, she shouted, "See you tomorrow, Charlie," and I had a feeling all that was about to change.

The First Day

....

Chapter 5

"It's your fault they make you uncomfortable, Sammie. You're the one with the crummy attitude," Charlie said as we hurried down Third Street to Beachside Middle School for our first day of school.

It was Monday morning at quarter to eight, and we were rushing. We had gotten a notice to go to the registration office to pick up our schedules before actual classes began. Ryan had left really early to meet with the volleyball coach, so Charlie and I were walking by ourselves. Even though we had done a test run with our dad to see how long it would take us to walk, it was taking longer than we had planned because we had to go up a really steep hill called the California Incline to get from the beach to the town of Santa Monica where the school was. Without our dad hustling us along, our pace had slowed down a bit.

"I'm telling you, Charlie," I answered, huffing and puffing, "you may think those kids are going to be your new, best friends, but they aren't like us. They're rich."

"How do you know? Just because their parents belong to a beach club?"

"A beach club where our dad *works*. Where we live in the *caretaker's bungalow*. Our family isn't a Sporty Forty. The Diamonds *work* for the Sporty Forties. We are not SF2 material."

"That is so paranoid, Sammie. To think that we can't be friends with those kids just because of that. They don't care what our parents do. Just try to be nice to them. You'll see. They'll be nice right back."

We had reached the entrance to the school, a big, white stucco building with a red, tile roof. Even though it was a public school, it looked like one of those California missions we had studied in fourth grade. Whoever built it had made it look really nice. Over the wide front door, it said *Beachside Middle School* in mosaic tiles. A flagpole stood on the front lawn and off to one side were about ten white bungalows that obviously had been added to house extra students. Parents' cars were lined up at the curb, dropping kids off in the carpool lane.

The first thing I noticed was how good everyone looked. At our old school, Culver City Middle School, we had to wear uniforms. Nothing horrible, but beige pants or skirts with a white top. The kids at Beachside were not only uniform-free, they looked like they stepped out of a fashion magazine. Even the sixth graders looked trendy. Lots of boys in surfer shorts and cool T-shirts. Lots of girls in sundresses or expensive jeans. I was in my regular jeans and a white top. When I was getting dressed, I decided to pick something that would blend in, but as I looked at the other girls, I wished I had worn a cute sundress like Charlie had.

We saw the General climbing out of a black Lexus and slinging his camouflage backpack over his shoulder. He looked over at us, and I thought about saluting, but decided against it. Charlie waved at him, and to my amazement, he smiled and waved back.

"See?" she said. "Just be friendly and the rest will happen naturally."

"Okay," I agreed. "That's fair. From this moment on, I will be nothing but nice, sweet, smiley Sammie."

"Good," she answered. "You look much better when you smile. Except for now, because you have a huge chunk of oatmeal in your teeth."

"Really?" I reached for my mouth to wipe the offensive chunk away, but nothing was there. Charlie just laughed.

"Very funny. Since when did you turn into Ryan?"

"I'm the dude," Charlie said, imitating Ryan. "I'm so *punny!*"

Charlie and I both cracked up as we walked into

the building and followed signs to the registration office. It felt good not to be angry at each other anymore. The Pizza Bonding had worked, just like it always had.

Inside the registration office was a counter with a tall, gray-haired woman standing behind it. There was a sign in front of her that said *I Can Only Please One Person a Day . . . and This Isn't Your Day.*

"We're here to pick up our schedules," Charlie said, getting right down to business. The woman didn't seem like someone you wanted to mess around with.

"We're Samantha and Charlotte Diamond," I added quickly.

"So you're twins?" the woman asked, rifling through a wooden box filled with printed, paper schedules. "Which one's older?"

Charlie and I glanced at each other and rolled our eyes. We have been asked that question a thousand million times. When people find out you're twins, it's the first thing they ask. Then they ask if you have a secret language. (By the way, we don't—although we both call Ryan "Ry Guy," and neither of us can pronounce *Massachusetts.* I don't think that qualifies as a secret language, though.)

"I'm older," Charlie said.

"But I'm wiser," I added.

We had given that same answer a thousand million times. It seemed to satisfy people so they could get right on to the secret language question.

"Well then, Older," the woman said, looking at Charlie, "here is your schedule. You have Ms. Hamel for homeroom. Room Thirteen, six doors down the main hall on your left. And you, Wiser," she added, looking at me, "you have Mr. Boring in Bungalow Three."

"Seriously?" I asked. "His name is Mr. Boring?"

Charlie and I could hardly contain our laughter.

"He's rather sensitive about it," the woman said. "So I suggest you get all your giggling about it over with now."

Then, in a tremendous surprise move, she leaned over the counter and whispered to us, "And the worst part is, he *is* a touch boring."

She put her hand over her mouth to stifle a laugh and returned to her desk behind the counter. We left the office to find Lauren and Brooke standing outside, their mouths hanging open.

"You're kidding me," Lauren said. "You guys were laughing with Mrs. Humphrey? She never laughs."

"Yeah," added Brooke. "All she ever does is mark you late and call your parents to say you're getting detention."

"It's funny you should bring this up," Charlie said. "Sammie and I were just saying that if you're nice to people, they'll be nice back. I guess it even works with Mrs. Humphrey. Right, Sammie?"

Oh, that's very subtle, Charlie. My happy face is on duty all day. I swear.

"Who do you have for homeroom?" Brooke asked Charlie.

"Ms. Hamel."

"Oh, that's my homeroom, too. Come on, I'll show you the way. Are you coming, Sammie?"

"Nope. I'm in Bungalow Three with Mr. Boring, who I'm told is."

I chuckled a little at my own joke.

"You're in my homeroom," Lauren said without so much as a hint of a smile. "I'll show you the way." She seemed a little disappointed that she got me instead of Charlie. I could understand that. I had been a pretty definite jerk to her.

Charlie and I compared schedules. We only had one class together, English with Ms. Carew. It was fifth period, right after lunch. That was great because we could go from lunch right to class together. Even though the school had a cafeteria, we had brought brown bags. Mine was a turkey sandwich, hold the mayo. I'm sure my dad had packed that himself.

Lauren and I said good-bye to Charlie and Brooke, then turned left into the school yard where the bungalows were. It was one minute to eight, and kids were hurrying to their classrooms so they wouldn't be late. Everyone said hi to Lauren as we crossed the yard.

"Listen, Lauren," I began, in between the enthusiastic *hi*s she was saying to every other person. "I want to apologize for asking you to leave yesterday.

I was just nervous about the tournament. There was a lot of pressure and everything."

"You were kind of a you-know-what that starts with a *b* and ends with an *h*."

"I know, and I'm really sorry."

"Apology accepted," Lauren said. "Your brother said you're not usually like that. He's such a great guy. Did he tell you we're hanging out after school today?"

"Yeah. Sure. Of course he did."

Actually, Ryan hadn't said a word about it. I don't know why I lied to Lauren, but something inside me just didn't want her to know more about Ryan than I did.

"I know he had to leave early this morning to meet the volleyball coach," she went on. "It's so exciting that they're recruiting him to be team captain."

"Really exciting," I agreed.

I didn't know Ryan had been asked to be team captain. I wondered when it happened that this girl who we'd only just met knew so much more about my family than I did.

We arrived in Bungalow 3 just as the bell rang. Spencer Whatshisname from the beach, wearing the same jeans and white T-shirt, called out to us. Well, actually, he called out to Lauren.

"Saved you a seat over here."

Lauren slid into the desk behind him, and I sat down at the desk in back of her.

And there we were: me in my new school, Lauren

Wadsworth, most beautiful girl, in front of me, and Spencer Whatshisname, handsome, popular dude, in front of her. Three cool ducks, all in a row.

This certainly hadn't been the way I expected it to go. But I was relieved that my transition to Beachside was turning out to be so easy.

Really, Sammie? If it's so easy, why are you sweating under your arms? You know you only do that when you're nervous.

I'm only going to tell you one thing about my homeroom: Mr. Boring was. And I mean *totally*. He spent the whole time going over our schedules—and not just our regular schedules, but assembly schedules, rainy-day schedules, and half-day schedules. He was obsessed with schedules. It was the most boring half hour of my entire life.

The only good thing about it was when I discovered that Alicia was in my homeroom. She was sitting on the other side of the room, talking to a couple of kids. One was a really tall, thin girl with wild, curly hair that puffed out in all directions. Even though it was hot outside, the girl was wearing high, lace-up, black boots. The other kid was a guy with red hair, but unlike Dan, the SF2 redhead who was tall and athletic, this guy was kind of round and had a pair of wooden drumsticks sticking out of his back pocket.

Hey, Alicia! I mouthed when Mr. Boring wasn't looking.

She smiled at me and mouthed the words *See you later.*

Lunch? I mouthed at her, and she nodded.

It was all set. Go to class. Meet up with Alicia for lunch. Ask Charlie to join us. Get to know each other. Maybe if Alicia lived nearby, the three of us could even stop at the Third Street Promenade on the way home.

Yup, it was going to be a great first day.

Lunch

....

Chapter 6

"We sit over there under the pavilion," Lauren told me as we wandered out to the yard after fourth period. "That's our table."

I had run into Lauren after Spanish while I was trying to get my new locker open. She held my backpack while I fiddled with the combination, which was a big help because I am not a gifted locker opener, and it took both hands and all my concentration to get the stupid thing open. I was actually very surprised that Lauren mentioned lunch to me, since I thought she had only invited Charlie to join them at their table. I said sure, I'd sit with them, knowing that Charlie would be extremely happy to see me keeping my promise about being friendly. I wanted to meet up with Alicia, too, but I figured I'd find her somewhere.

The cafeteria at Beachside is indoors, but you have your choice of eating inside or outside. It smells like cafeteria food inside, so if the weather is good, which it almost always is, most kids choose to eat outside. The best tables are located under the pavilion, which is this green, metal tent-kind-of-thing that provides a shady area so you don't have to sit out in the hot sun to eat. It's also the area closest to the cafeteria, so kids can buy a hot lunch or pick up something from the quick-serve window and then just head outside to their table. Of course, the SF2 table was under the pavilion, right smack in the center. The best spot for seeing and being seen.

As I followed Lauren over to their table, I saw that the whole area was swarming with kids. Some were lined up in the cafeteria with trays, waiting to pay for their lunches. Most of the others were buying a sandwich or a yogurt at one of the two quick-serve windows. I noticed there weren't many kids with brown-bag lunches. Almost everyone at my old school brought their lunch, but it didn't seem to be the thing to do at Beachside. I made a mental note of that.

Uncool Thing Number One: Brown bags.

Uncool Thing Number Two: That lip gloss smudge I am just noticing over my right boob. How did I manage to get lip gloss there of all places? It looks like I kissed my own chest.

I tried to rub out the glossy, pink splotch over my boob without Lauren noticing. Needing a little privacy for this move, I purposely lagged a little behind her as we passed the tables farthest away from the pavilion. It was where the sixth graders sat. I had just been in sixth grade last year, but suddenly those kids looked so young to me. There they were, making a ton of noise, talking with food in their mouths, the boys and the girls sitting at separate tables. And suddenly, here I was, going to the best table at the school, where good-looking boys and pretty girls sat side by side and talked about music and movies and parties. I confess, I felt extremely cool—well, except for the mess going on over my right boob. That was definitely not cool.

When we reached the table, I sat down next to Lauren.

"Oh, that's so cute," Lauren said, noticing the brown bag I placed on the table. "I used to bring my lunch when I was little. My mom would put applesauce in those little Tupperware thingies."

I closed my eyes and prayed that I had no little Tupperware thingies in there. It was bad enough that I had the bag. I reached in and pulled out a turkey sandwich on wheat (in a plastic bag) and a nectarine.

Thank you, oh protector of the nerds, for saving me the embarrassment of random Tupperware thingies.

One by one, the SF2s gathered at the table. Ben, of plaid pants and glasses fame, arrived first. I learned from listening to his conversation with Lauren that his name was Ben Feldman, he was turning thirteen in

November, and he was having his bar mitzvah party at Dodger Stadium.

"You're kidding," I said to him. "You're taking over a whole baseball stadium?"

"I wish," he said. "We're just renting the restaurant there called the Stadium Club. Still, it's a pretty cool place. You'll see."

I will? Does that mean I'm invited? Oh wow, since when did I become a popular girl?

I was still racking my brains for the next thing to say to Ben when Jillian arrived, full of complaints and conversation. Complaints about how stupid it was to have to study different weather systems in science because, really, she was never leaving California where it was sunny all the time. And conversation about which reality show was her favorite: *Real Teens, Teen Beauty Secrets,* or *Teen Chefs.* (I'll spare you the details, but you probably won't be surprised to know that *Teen Beauty Secrets* won big-time.)

I was so relieved to see Charlie coming out of the main building and walking to our table. As much as I was flattered to sit at the SF2 table, I really wasn't comfortable with them and was dying for my sister to get there. She was walking between Jared and two other guys in long basketball shorts. Lauren whispered to me that they were the stars of the seventh-grade basketball team. In fact, Sean, the guy on the left with the buzzed, black hair, played three sports—soccer, basketball, and baseball—and was

All-City in all three. I was extremely intimidated when he slid onto the bench next to me.

"Hey, your sister says you guys are awesome tennis players," he said, unwrapping his sub and taking a giant bite almost before he had finished the sentence. "I'm starving."

"We were ranked players last year," I said. "We're still working on getting our Under-Fourteen ranking, but it's much harder than . . ."

I stopped talking midstream because I realized Sean wasn't listening. In fact, he had turned his back to me and was grabbing a bag of chips from Jared while fake-punching him in the stomach.

"Gimme some of those, punk. I love those barbecue ones. Crave 'em, man."

I looked down and took a bite of my turkey sandwich like it was the thing I most wanted to do in the world. I was desperate to look like I didn't care at all that Sean had turned his back on me.

Between you and me and the turkey sandwich, that couldn't have been less true.

Charlie sat down across from me.

"Hey, Sammie. Did your morning go okay?"

"Fine. I couldn't understand anything my Spanish teacher said, but we got to pick Spanish names for ourselves, and I chose Guacamole."

I thought Charlie would laugh because I myself thought it was hilarious to be called Guacamole. But she didn't laugh. I could see her eyeing my turkey sandwich and nectarine. She shook her head disapprovingly.

"Sammie Diamond, get rid of those," she whispered, and nodded her head in the direction of the trash can.

"But I'm hungry."

"Eat later. Nobody else here has a bag lunch. Do it now, Sammie, when no one is looking."

She turned to Sean and Jared and distracted them with her A-plus smile as I slid out from the table and shuffled as inconspicuously as I could over to the trash can. I was just about to toss my lunch in when I felt a hand on my shoulder.

"Hey, girl, I've been looking for you." It was Alicia. She was standing next to the tall girl with the poofy hair and black boots. "Sammie, meet my friend Sara Berlin. Berlin. Bermudez. Get it? We sat next to each other all through grammar school."

"Back in the good, old days of alphabetical seating," Sara said. "We had this teacher named Mr. Oscar—remember him, Allie? We used to call him Oscar the Grouch. He looked like this."

Sara crossed her eyes and puffed up her cheeks and pulled some of her poofy hair over her upper lip to look like a mustache.

"Children, shame on you!" she said in a gravelly, male-type voice. "You are acting like children again!"

Alicia cracked up, and I did, too. Even though I had never met Mr. Oscar, I knew exactly what he looked and sounded like.

"Charlie and I had this fourth-grade teacher named Mrs. Fish," I said, when I had recovered from laughing. "And she looked just like one. No kidding."

I sucked in my cheeks and made my famous fish face, which I had spent the whole fourth grade perfecting. I can even make a little bubble-blowing sound when I do it. Alicia and Sara burst into laughter.

Just then, Ryan walked up to us. "Hey, Sammie. I saw you doing your Mrs. Fish imitation. I haven't seen that in a long time. It's ace."

He turned to Alicia and Sara. "Hello, girls. I don't know if you're aware of it, but Sammie here can do an amazing imitation of a baby. Show them, Sam-I-Am."

"It's nothing," I said. "No big deal."

"No, we want to see," Alicia said.

"Okay, but it's definitely silly."

"Definitely silly is how we roll," Sara said.

I held my nose and stuck my tongue out and squinched up my eyes so you could hardly see them and made this little baby wail. I don't know how I learned to do it, but what comes out of my mouth truly sounds like a baby. Once I was practicing it in the stall of a bathroom at school, and somebody called the principal because they thought someone had left a baby there.

"That's unbelievable," Alicia said, holding her sides from laughing. "How'd you learn to do that?"

"I'll let you in on a little secret," Ryan said. "She really *is* a baby. Don't tell anyone, but she still sucks her thumb at night."

"I do not!" I protested, but it didn't matter, because Alicia and Sara didn't believe him, anyway. They were both laughing and giving Ryan flirty looks. It's amazing. He is a total girl magnet without even trying.

"You're both such naturals," Sara said. "Really talented." Then, turning to Alicia, she added, "We should get them to come to Truth Tellers."

"Truth Tellers?" Ryan said. "Whoa, that sounds serious. What is it?"

"It's this kind of drama group that meets after school," Alicia said. "Sara and I are in it, and a bunch of our other friends."

"You do plays?" I asked.

"No, it's not that kind of drama. We do sketches and monologues and scenes about our lives. We try to tell the truth about things, 'express our true selves,' as Ms. Carew says. She's our sponsor."

I recognized her name from my schedule. "Oh, she's my English teacher. Can anyone join?"

"Anyone who's interested."

"Well, that leaves me out," Ryan said. "No offense, ladies, but it sounds way too weird for me. My true self doesn't have all that much to say."

"What about you, Sammie?" Sara asked.

Before I could answer, I heard Lauren's voice next to me. I hadn't seen her approach, but apparently she had just come from the quick-service window because she was holding two peach yogurts.

"I got you some lunch," she said to Ryan. "You coming to our table?"

"Sure," Ryan said. "You didn't happen to get a cheeseburger or anything, did you? Not that yogurt doesn't look delish, but I'm what you call a meat eater."

"Well, come on, meat eater," she said, flashing him a strawberry-scented smile. "Someone at the table will have some caveman food. Let's go. You coming, Sammie?"

What I wanted to do was stay there with Alicia and Sara. It was so easy to be with them. We were having fun. I hadn't realized how much energy I was exerting to talk with all the kids at the SF2 table until I felt how easy and natural it was to be with these other girls. I didn't feel like they were judging me. We were just all being us.

"Come on, Sammie," Lauren repeated as she and Ryan walked away.

All right, Sammie. Stand up for yourself. Tell her you're not going to the SF2 table. Tell her those kids make your armpits sweat.

"Hey, Lauren," I called out. "I think I'm going to—"

Lauren turned around, interrupting me. "Sammie. Everybody's waiting."

I stood there for a second, and then I made a decision. Actually, it wasn't even a decision; it was more of a reflex, the kind of thing you do before you even have a chance to think about it.

I went. I don't know why, but I did.

I said a quick good-bye to Alicia and Sara and followed Lauren to the table. When I got there, I sat down next to Ryan, who promptly announced that I would do my baby imitation in exchange for somebody giving him something with meat in it. Jared gave him half of his second meatball sub and I was on.

"Do it, Sammie," Ryan urged. "You guys, this is going to blow you away. Watch this."

I held my nose, stuck out my tongue, squinched up my eyes, and let out one of the funnier baby wails I have ever done.

But you know what?

No one laughed.

Ms. Carew

....

Chapter 7

"Now that you've had a week to adjust to the new school year, we are happy to announce that after-school activities will begin today," Principal Pfeiffer said over the loudspeaker. "The Chess Club meets in Room Fourteen with Mrs. Zajak, the Film Club in the auditorium with Mr. Walsh, the debate team in Bungalow Three with Mr. Boring, and Truth Tellers in the Patio Room with Ms. Carew. Los Amigos meet in Room Six with Senor Zaragoza, and Study Hall is open in the library until four thirty."

I was sitting in homeroom, trying to finish a Spanish worksheet that I hadn't completed over the weekend. Since Charlie and I were playing in another tournament the next weekend, Dad had us practicing nonstop, which meant we had to leave all our homework until Sunday night. Wouldn't you know it, that was the night GoGo had asked Charlie and me out for sushi. Charlie said no because Lauren was calling to review the science project they were working on together. I said my homework was all done, which it wasn't, and went with GoGo to her favorite sushi restaurant where you can sit at the counter and watch the sushi chefs carve cucumbers into fans and carrots into flowers.

While we were waiting for our sushi combo to be delivered, I told GoGo all about school: about the SF2s, about our lunch table, about Alicia and Sara and the Truth Tellers group they belonged to. I had been thinking about that club all week. It seemed so different from anything I had ever done, yet somehow it really interested me.

"That sounds like something I did in college," GoGo said. "It's called improvisation, and it's kind of drama, but you make things up as you go along. We did exercises that taught us to express ourselves. I found it to be excellent preparation for my career."

"But, GoGo, you design jewelry. I don't see how making stuff up in front of an audience helps you make silver earrings and bracelets."

"Anything you do that frees the mind and heightens your creativity is good for you, Sammie."

"But the kids in this group, they're kind of weird. I mean, I like Alicia a lot, but some of her friends are—"

"Let me stop you right there, my darling granddaughter. If there's one thing I can teach you, it's to have an open mind. Some of the most interesting people I've met might be considered weird, but when I got to know them, I found them fascinating."

"Was Grandpa weird?"

"No." She sighed. "Maybe that's why we divorced."

After that, the sushi came, and while we ate I tried to explain to her how Charlie and I had become friends with the SF2s and how they'd all think it was geeky if I joined Truth Tellers. She said exactly what I knew she'd say.

"Follow your heart, my darling. That's the only sure road to happiness I know."

Not so easy when you have a sister who's obsessed with becoming friends with Lauren Wadsworth.

"Is that what you taught Mom, GoGo? To follow her heart?"

"It is. And finally she got the courage to go to culinary school and follow her dream of opening a restaurant."

"I miss her."

"Of course you do," GoGo said, giving my hand a squeeze. "But when she returns, she'll be complete. She'll have her beautiful family and work she loves. Who could ask for more?"

But back to homeroom. As Principal Pfeiffer read the list of after-school activities, I found myself writing down *Truth Tellers, Patio Room*. Just in case. Lauren, who was sitting at the desk next to mine, saw me do it and shook her head.

"Don't even think about it," she whispered. "It's not for us. Besides, we're going to the Third Street Promenade after school. I got a gift card to Starbucks for my birthday, so the Frappuccinos are on me!"

It was amazing how quickly Charlie and I were becoming accepted by the kids from the Sporty Forty. Over the weekend, Lauren and Brooke had come to the club with their parents and stopped by the courts to watch us practice. Of course, it probably didn't hurt that Ryan was hitting with us. Every time he made a good shot, he'd toss his racket up in the air and catch it by the handle, and Lauren would jump up and down like a cheerleader. She had a supermassive crush on him. Jared and Sean came to the beach with us to do some boogie boarding, and afterward, we all sat around and had chips and dip.

Oh, I know what you're thinking. Don't worry, I had veggies and dip. No chips for Miss One Two Six and a Half.

"I think it's great that you girls are making such nice friends," Dad had said at dinner that night. "It makes me think we did the right thing by moving to the club."

Charlie smiled happily. "I love it here. And I love Beachside. I didn't know school could be so fun."

There was a silence and Dad looked over at me.

"You feel the same way, Sammie?"

I hesitated. Then I glanced over at Charlie. She was waiting for my answer.

"Sure," I said. "What's not to like?"

Both Charlie and my dad seemed happy with that answer. "I think living at the Sporty Forty is good for your game, too," he went on. "Lots of court time. I'm predicting good things for the tournament this weekend. That is, if a certain someone can keep her focus."

I didn't answer or look up, just concentrated on not taking a second portion of mashed potatoes.

Later that night as we crawled into our beds and switched off the lights, Charlie turned to me with a big smile.

"I'm really feeling like a teenager now," she said. "It's so awesome, isn't it? At Culver, I felt like a little kid. We never talked to boys unless we were playing tennis with them. And I didn't even know what a Starbucks was."

And then, just the very next day, we would be going with Lauren, Brooke, Jillian, and Lily for Frappuccinos at Starbucks. Charlie was right. Things had changed fast; so fast I hardly knew where I was.

The only class I shared with Charlie was fifth period English. Lauren and Lily were in class with us, too, so after lunch at "our table," the four of us always walked over to Ms. Carew's classroom together. It was called the Patio Room because it had sliding, glass doors that opened onto a little, red-tiled outside area.

"I found the greatest dress over the weekend," Lily said as we walked. "I got it at the Salvation Army store for only three dollars."

"Ewww," Lauren said. "I can't believe you bought an ABW dress."

"Who's ABW?" Charlie asked cautiously. "A hot designer I haven't heard of yet?"

Yet? Like you know a whole lot about hot designers? We are the girls who wear tennis skorts, remember?

"ABW stands for Already Been Worn." Lauren frowned as she said the words. "None of us can believe that Lily doesn't mind wearing other people's toss-outs."

"I prefer to call them vintage clothes," Lily explained. "If you add a cool belt or some cowboy boots or interesting jewelry, you get your own look. Not like the Gap stuff that everyone else is wearing."

"I think that's great," I said.

"Well, I think it's unsanitary," Lauren snapped back.

Before Lily could answer, we had reached the Patio Room.

Our English teacher, Ms. Carew, had become my

favorite teacher over the course of the first week, not that Mr. Boring with his daily reading of school rules gave her much competition. She was young and pretty, with close-cropped black hair and big, colorful earrings that were made in Africa. She had been to Africa over the summer to try to find her ancestors there, but she said she had better luck finding earrings.

"Hello, girls." Ms. Carew greeted us with a warm smile as we walked into class.

"Great earrings," Lily said as she passed by. Today Ms. Carew was wearing long, dangling, yellow-and-black, beaded ones.

"Right back at you," Ms. Carew said, noticing the hoop earrings Lily was wearing that looked like a snake coiled up into a circle.

"They're ABW earrings," Lauren remarked.

"The best kind," Ms. Carew answered.

Every day, Ms. Carew wrote a thought for the day on the board. I liked reading them. As we took our seats, she went to the board and wrote *Success is liking yourself, liking what you do, and liking how you do it*. I liked that quote and wrote it down on the inside cover of my notebook.

"Our thought for the day is from the American poet Maya Angelou," Ms. Carew said after the bell rang. "And we're going to use this quote as the basis for our writing assignment."

"Ick," Charlie whispered to me. She hated writing assignments. Unlike me, she loved subjects like math, where your grade was based on how many answers you got right or wrong. When we did our homework together, I always helped her with her writing, and she helped me with my math. Like our dad always says, we're two halves of a circle.

"I have an interesting assignment for you today," Ms. Carew was saying as she walked up and down the aisles, handing out a sheet of pale-green paper. "On one side of this paper, I want you to write one thing you like about yourself. On the flip side, write one thing you don't like about yourself. Write something that you feel comfortable sharing with your classmates."

"What's this have to do with English?" Sean called out.

"English involves learning to be writers," Ms. Carew said. "You can't be a writer unless you understand yourself first."

"Is this graded?" the General wanted to know.

"No, Dwayne. This is an exercise in understanding, not in judging."

"His name is Dwayne!" I whispered to Charlie.

"No wonder he calls himself the General," she whispered back, and we cracked up.

Ms. Carew turned out the fluorescent lights and asked us to reach inside of ourselves and tell the truth. I had never had an assignment like that. Mr. Yamazaki, my last English teacher, was always too worked up about proper punctuation to care about what we were actually writing. As long as it had the commas in the right place, he was happy. Give the guy a semicolon, and he was over the moon. So I had to really think hard about what I wanted to say. It was easy to think of what I like least about myself, which I believe we all know is my weight. What I like best about myself was much harder to think of.

After a few minutes, Ms. Carew turned on the lights and had us go out onto the little patio that adjoined her room. My old school certainly didn't have any patios where students could meet outside, but Beachside was a beautiful campus with all sorts of tucked-away green spaces. We sat down in a circle on the red tiles and read what we had written. Ms. Carew said no one was allowed to comment. She told us to just listen, and listen with our hearts.

When she said that, one of the boys made a farting sound with his mouth, and a couple of his buddies laughed, including the General and Jared and Sean. Ms. Carew frowned at them and told them there would be none of that in her class. She said we were there to be true friends and writing partners, and no one was to make fun of anyone else.

She called on Charlie to go first. I was so grateful that she didn't pick me.

Charlie said the thing she liked most about herself was her tennis stroke—forehand, of course, because her backhand was inconsistent. It sounded like my dad had invaded her brain like some alien creature in a sci-fi movie! Then she turned into the real Charlie, saying what she liked least were her toes, because her third toe was longer than her second toe and she felt toes should go in descending order. She looked over at me for approval, and I gave her our secret love sign, three taps on the chest right over your heart.

The redheaded guy with the drumsticks in his pocket (whose name, I learned, was Bernard) said he liked his rhythm best. And the thing he liked least—well, it was a tie between his cheeks and his freckles, so he was going with both. Lily said the thing she liked best was her knack for doing creative things with belts. And the thing she liked least was that she bites her nails when she is nervous. Alicia's friend Sara, who wasn't wearing her boots but was wearing some equally strange sandals decorated with seashells, said what she liked best was her hair. That was amazing to me, since her hair looked like someone had whipped it up with an egg beater. And what she liked least was that she gets impatient with her little brother, who has autism. Wow, that was a brave thing to say. A guy named Devon said what he liked best was his swagger. And the thing he liked least was that, deep down, he actually liked Lady Gaga's music.

It was an amazing experience. Everyone was really trying to be honest and deep. Well, everyone but Lauren Wadsworth, that is. She said the thing she liked best about herself was the way her hair looked just after she washed it. And the thing she liked least was that she could never decide which tank top to wear under which shirt. And, of course, there was Sean, who said the thing he liked best was his collection of All-City trophies, and the thing he liked least was nothing.

Way to be humble, Sean.

We continued around the circle until we came to the last person to read—me.

"The thing I like best about myself is that I make myself laugh," I read. Then I flipped the paper over and saw what I had written for what I liked least about myself. It said *The thing I like least about myself is that I am messy.*

Let's be honest here, Sammie. You know that's not true. Tell the truth, girlfriend. Try it, maybe you'll like it.

The truth was too scary and too personal. I wasn't about to tell these people that I weighed one two six and a half. No, I was going with what I had written. I looked down at the paper and started to read.

"The thing I like least about myself . . ." Then I paused and glanced up to see Ms. Carew looking at me. She seemed so interested, and her eyes were . . . I don't know . . . curious, like she really cared what I was about to say. I don't know what got into me, but I took a deep breath and said the truth.

"The thing I like least about myself is . . . well . . . it's too private to say here."

There it was: not a lie, but not the truth, either.

"Hey, that's cheating," Sean called out. "Everyone else spilled their guts. Like me, about the trophies and everything."

Ms. Carew held up her hand for him to stop talking. "What you did is perfectly okay, Sammie," she said. "People reveal themselves when they're ready."

Phew.

Before we went back in the classroom, Ms. Carew asked us, "Does anyone remember our quote for the day? About the true meaning of success?"

Before I knew it, my hand shot up in the air.

"'Success is liking yourself, liking what you do, and liking how you do it,'" I said, surprising myself that I had memorized every word.

"Very nice, Sammie," Ms. Carew said, and I noticed Lauren Wadsworth look over at Charlie and roll her eyes.

When the bell rang and I got up to leave, Ms. Carew pulled me aside.

"Can I see you a second, Sammie?"

"Sure."

"Alicia and Sara tell me they think you might be interested in Truth Tellers," she began.

I looked out the door and saw Lauren in the hall, mouthing the word *Frappuccino.*

"I have a lot of stuff to do after school," I told Ms. Carew. "I don't think I can make it."

"You're always welcome, Sammie," she said. "And even if you don't decide to join us, here's a copy of a poem by Sonya Sones, one of my favorite poets. I'd love for you to have it."

"Thanks a lot, Ms. Carew. But I have to go to my next class."

I grabbed the piece of paper and ran out the door.

"What was that about?" Lily asked.

"She wants me to proofread my stuff more carefully," I lied. "Check out the commas and everything."

"That Ms. Carew is so old-school," Lauren said. "I mean, really, what do you like best about yourself?"

I wanted to defend Ms. Carew, but I knew Charlie wouldn't like it if I made a fuss about disagreeing with Lauren. So I didn't say anything, just listened as Lauren launched into a conversation about where we were going to meet after school for our Starbucks date. It was agreed that we'd meet at the flagpole and walk over to the mall together.

Then we went our separate ways. I had to hurry to get to my math class on time.

As Mr. Warner was having kids write their homework answers on the board, I pulled out the poem that Ms. Carew had given me after class. At the top of the page, it said "'Fantabulous' by Sonya Sones." I started to read.

I don't need to rock
a pair of size 2 jeans
or prance through the pages
of magazines

because I am a woman
who's round and full,
made of wind and wild
and honey.

A woman made
of curve and swerve
and flow and glow
and strong and funny.

I am a woman made
of fire and fierce and free.
I am fantabulous.
Fantabulous me!

I couldn't believe what I was reading. It was fantastic. Amazing. I'm not much of a poem reader except for those funny *Where the Sidewalk Ends* poems my mom read us when we were little. But this poem—wow. It was like the words reached out and grabbed me.

I am a woman made of fire and fierce and free.

I read those lines over and over again. It was like Sonya Sones, wherever she was, had looked inside me and picked out just the words I needed to hear. I couldn't stop staring at that poem—it made me feel so good about myself. I didn't even mind when Mr. Warner got angry because I didn't seem interested in learning how to convert fractions to decimals.

Oh no, Mr. Warner. I'm fascinated by fraction-to-decimal conversions. Oh, and by the way, did you know I'm fantabulous?

This might sound totally corny, and I apologize if it does, but when I read that poem, I felt like I was floating on air, free as a seagull. It's strange. I felt like maybe it set loose someone inside me, a person I didn't know, who had been waiting to get out. I didn't know who she was, but I had a feeling she was fantabulous, and I wanted to meet her.

Truth Tellers

....

Chapter 8

"What do you mean, you're not going to Starbucks?" Charlie demanded, putting her hands on her hips the way she does when she gets mad. "We're *all* going."

We were standing at the flagpole after school that day, waiting for the SF2 girls to join us for our Starbucks date.

"I'm not thirsty," I said.

"Sammie, since when does thirst have anything to do with Starbucks?"

"Earth to Charlie. It's a place for drinks, as in, 'I'm thirsty, I want a drink.'"

"It's a place for hanging out, Sammie. Everyone knows that."

"Okay, so the truth is," I said reluctantly, "I

don't want to go because I'm thinking of trying the club that Ms. Carew runs."

"You mean that truth-talker thing?"

"Truth Tellers. It's Truth Tellers, not talkers."

"Whatever. Why, Sammie? We're not drama people. We're athletes. We're not like those alternative kids who sit around and fall in love with their every little thought."

"You don't know that's what they're like, Charlie. I just think it might be interesting, that's all. Alicia says it's really fun. And Ms. Carew is great."

"Sammie, we've always liked the same things, right? So I don't get it. We don't have anything in common with those kids. Alicia is cool, but what about that friend of hers with the boots and crazy hair?"

"Her name is Sara Berlin. That's not fair, Charlie, and you know it. You can't judge someone just by looking at what they're wearing or how good their hair looks. Oh, and speaking of good hair, here come Lily, Brooke, and Lauren."

"Please don't tell them about this truth-club thing," Charlie whispered. "I don't want to have to explain you to them. Just do what you have to do and don't say anything."

Lauren, Lily, and Brooke were running down the school steps to where we were waiting at the flagpole. Jogging alongside them in his usual camouflage cargo pants was the General, whose full name, Charlie told me, was Dwayne Dickerson. Their history teacher, who apparently calls everyone by their last name, would only call him Mr. Dickerson since he said he didn't think it was appropriate to call him the General. He said there were real generals that actually deserved the title.

"Excellent news, girls," Brooke said when they reached us. "The guys are going to hang out with us at Starbucks."

"I only see one guy," I said.

"But I bet you like what you see," the General answered, striking a muscleman pose.

Oh, please. Don't tell me you think that's flirty, because honestly, you look like a G.I. Joe action figure with arm cramps.

"Jared and Sean and Spencer are on the track running some laps for the coach," the General explained. "I'll grab them when they're done and we'll all come by."

"Eeuuwww," said Lauren. "Make sure they shower first. I hate sweaty people."

"Yeah, it's so gross," Charlie agreed.

Whoa. Did Charlie actually say that? In front of me, the person who sweats so much, she actually produced a leg trickle at the last tennis tournament?

"Sweating is a very natural thing," I said in my own defense. "It's the body's way of cooling off."

"That's very scientific," Lauren commented.

"And oh-so-boring," Brooke added. "No offense, Sammie."

Everyone laughed. Yes, even Charlie!

"Listen, everyone," I said. "Don't all cry at once, but I'm not going to be able to make it to Starbucks. I have . . . um . . . other plans."

"Really?" asked Lily. "What are you doing?"

Charlie jumped in before I could answer. "She has an orthodontist appointment."

"Then how come *you* don't have one?" the General asked her. "You're identical. You should have identical teeth."

"Yes, we do . . . except . . . Sammie has an extra one."

I do? Since when?

"Like a fang?" the General asked. "Cool! Can I see it?"

"No way," I snapped at him.

"You can't see it without looking really hard," Charlie chimed in. "It's a molar, in the back. No one knows where it came from, and it's got to be pulled or it will just keep growing until it's, like, superlong."

"Eeuuwww, gross," Lauren said again, trying not to look at my mouth. "You poor thing."

Thanks, Charlie. Now everyone can truly feel sorry for me—Sammie the overweight tooth freak.

I said good-bye and watched as the four of them took off across the lawn. Just before they reached the sidewalk and headed down Third Street, Charlie turned around and shot me a peculiar look. It's funny—I couldn't tell from her expression whether she was happy or sad.

"Hey, Sam. Are you sure you can't come?" she yelled. Then, realizing what she had said, she added, "I could get Dad to cancel the appointment."

"It's okay," I yelled back. "Maybe I can swing by later, depending on how long my . . . um . . . appointment goes."

Charlie nodded and waved good-bye.

Love you, she mouthed, giving me three little taps over her heart.

"Love you, too," I whispered, and tapped my chest three times.

And then she disappeared around the corner. I had a funny feeling in the pit of my stomach. We were only going to be a few blocks from each other, but as I headed back to Ms. Carew's room, I felt that a distance had begun to open up between Charlie and me. And to be honest, I didn't like that feeling one bit.

The door was closed when I reached the Patio Room, but I could hear voices coming from inside. It sounded like buzzing as if a bunch of bees had gotten loose and were swarming. I pushed the door open a crack. There were about fifteen kids inside. The desks had been pushed against the walls so the center of the room was empty, and the kids were sitting in a circle on the floor with their eyes closed. They were humming.

Yup, humming. What was that all about?

Ms. Carew noticed me at the door and came over to greet me.

"Good to see you here, Sammie," she said quietly, not wanting to interrupt the swarm of bees. "Do you want to join our acceptance circle?"

"No, thanks. I'm not a very good hummer."

That was bogus. I can actually hum up a storm, but usually I do it in the shower or when I'm working on my scrapbook, not in a group of people I don't know. I was beginning to feel like I had come to the wrong place, that I really belonged at Starbucks with Charlie and the SF2s.

Ms. Carew laughed. "It's a warm-up exercise. We hum to get used to the sounds of our voices in the room. That makes us more comfortable when we speak."

"Why do you call it an acceptance circle?"

"Because everyone in the circle accepts each person for exactly who they are. That's the only requirement to join this group."

"Wow. That's . . . um . . . different."

"In Truth Tellers, we welcome difference. We embrace it," Ms. Carew explained.

So, like, this is a place where I could bring my brown-bag turkey sandwich and nectarine and no one will think I'm a total geek? Amazing.

I followed Ms. Carew over to the circle of kids and took a seat on the floor. I'll be honest: I felt extremely uncomfortable. I wasn't into public humming, and even though they were wrapping that part up, I didn't know what to expect next.

"Everyone, this is Sammie Diamond," Ms. Carew said, taking her seat in the circle. "She's thinking about joining our group. Sammie, why don't you tell us something about yourself."

I looked around the circle. Alicia was there, of course, and Sara, too. Alicia was wearing another beautiful, embroidered shirt, which I assumed was from El Salvador, and Sara had pulled her hair back with a rubber band so it looked like a giant, poofy French poodle tail. Bernard, Mr. Drumsticks, was sitting next to Devon, the secret Lady Gaga fan from my English class.

Other than that, I didn't know any of the kids, but I noticed two things about them all. One, they seemed very relaxed. And two, they had taken their shoes off and were sitting there in their bare feet. I wondered why. Maybe you can't lie about yourself when your feet are exposed. Or maybe a person's truth center is located in their toes. Or what if it had to do with socks, like they just keep you all bottled up inside? Or perhaps it was—

"Sammie," I heard Ms. Carew saying. Oops—I had gotten carried away with the foot-and-sock-truth thing and checked out completely.

"Yes?" I said, coming back to earth.

"You were going to tell us something about yourself."

"Oh, right. Well, I'm a good tennis player. And I just moved here from Culver City. And I'm a twin. Those are the basics."

"Does anyone have any questions they'd like to ask Sammie?" Ms. Carew asked the group.

Here it comes, I thought. *The twin questions, just like always. Which one of you is older? And do you have a secret language?*

Unbelievably, no one asked either of those. They asked about me, and their questions were the most fun questions I'd ever been asked.

"If you had to do one or the other for an hour, would you rather hop or skip?" a small sixth-grader named Will Lee asked.

"Hop, for sure." I laughed. "I never actually learned to skip."

"What's your favorite word?" Bernard asked.

That was easy. "*Fantabulous.* I just learned it today. It means *marvelously good.*"

I smiled shyly at Ms. Carew.

"What's your favorite word in Spanish?" Alicia asked.

"*Guacamole.*"

"Mine's *corazón,*" Alicia commented. "It means *heart.*"

"What's the most disgusting thing you can think of?" a girl named Etta asked. She had a green streak in her spiky, black hair.

"My brother, Ryan."

She raised her eyebrows. "The hot eighth-grade guy?"

"Everyone thinks he's hot, but he flosses his teeth at the dinner table, which is totally disgusting. Oops—maybe I shouldn't have said that. It's kind of personal."

"This is a safe place," Ms. Carew said. "What we say in here stays in here."

"What's the funniest sound you can make?" Sara asked. "And I think I already know the answer."

I held my nose, squinched up my face, and did the baby cry. I don't know what got into me, but it wasn't just one cry. It was a total baby temper tantrum, with sobs, gags, snivels—the whole thing. I was feeling so loose with this group, it didn't even occur to me to hold back. It was only after I finished that I realized the extended tantrum might have been a little much, even for the alternative kids.

But it was the opposite. Everyone laughed and clapped and cheered and said things like "amazing," "hilarious," and "a total crack-up."

Ms. Carew explained that now that we were warmed up and ready to share, we were going to do a truth-telling exercise. She would say a feeling, and anyone who wanted could tell about a time when they felt that emotion. She could see I was a little uncomfortable with that, so she said that I could just listen, that listening with your heart was the best kind of sharing.

"The emotion for today is frightened," Ms. Carew began. "Tell us about a time when you were frightened."

Everyone was silent until Alicia spoke up.

"I came to this country when I was three years old, hidden in the back of my uncle's car," she said. "I remember stopping at the Mexican border and seeing the American guard. He had blond hair and a blond mustache—I had never seen anyone with yellow hair, and I thought he was an alien. He shined a flashlight in my face and yelled at me in a language I couldn't understand. I was so frightened! I thought they were going to take me away from my parents. I still have nightmares about it."

Other kids spoke after that, but I couldn't stop thinking about Alicia's story. I wondered if anyone else at school knew what she had been through. It's amazing what we don't know about people.

That's what I kept thinking as I listened to each person's story. Will Lee was frightened when he had to show his parents his report card with a B in math. They were from Korea, and it was really important to them that their son get straight As so he would do well in their new country. Devon was frightened every time he came up to bat and had to face a new pitcher. Sara told about a time when they couldn't find her little brother and searched all over the house and finally found him sitting on a curb half a block away. Bernard was frightened in PE because he didn't want to change his clothes in front of everyone. Etta was frightened on her first day of eighth grade because she didn't know if people would make fun of her hair. A seventh-grader named Keisha said she was frightened the first time she kissed a boy for real, because she didn't know if she was doing it right.

By the time they had gone around the circle, I felt like we were all old friends. The hour had whizzed by, and as we left the room, everyone was laughing and talking.

I asked Alicia if she wanted to walk home together. I just assumed she was walking to the Sporty Forty so her dad could drive her home, but she said that she usually took the bus after school. She lived about an hour away. She went to Beachside because her mom and dad worked in the district and got her a special permit.

We walked to the bus stop on Third Street and Arizona Avenue, right in front of the Third Street Promenade. I told Alicia that I was pretty sure I was going to join Truth Tellers. She was glad and told me about these performances that they sometimes did for the community. The last one was at the Laugh Box, a comedy club. Over one hundred people came, and they weren't all just parents, either.

"I can't imagine standing up in front of grown-ups and telling them for real about my life," I said.

"Once you do it, it's really fun. At our last performance, this woman told me she hadn't really thought about how it feels to be twelve, and what I said helped her to understand her daughter. That was cool."

We were so busy talking that I hadn't noticed that we had reached the bus stop in front of the mall—specifically, in front of Starbucks. And, of course, who should see us but Charlie and Lauren and the other SF2s who were sitting around an outside table. I was supposed to be at the dentist getting my fang pulled, and it was clear to everyone that I wasn't. I think we can all agree that the situation was totally, completely, horribly awkward.

"Hey, Sammie. What are you doing here?" Lauren called out. I could see Charlie burying her face in her hands.

"She doesn't look like a dentist," the General shouted, pointing to Alicia. "But if she were, I'd go more often."

"That guy thinks he's such hot stuff," Alicia whispered. "And why does he think I'm a dentist?"

I was really embarrassed to have to confess to Alicia that I hid the fact that I was going to Truth Tellers. I was tempted to tell her something different, but then I realized that if I was going to be a Truth Teller, I was going to have to start telling the truth. That was the deal.

"I'll be right over, guys!" I hollered to the kids at the

table. Then I took a deep breath and turned to Alicia.

"I didn't tell them I was going to Truth Tellers," I said. "I told them I had a dentist appointment."

"Why?" she asked. She seemed really confused.

"My sister asked me not to tell them about Truth Tellers. She didn't want them to think I was a geek. We're just getting to know them, and she wants to make a good impression."

I watched Alicia's face carefully. I could see her shaking her head sadly, fighting back tears. At last she spoke.

"So your sister is embarrassed that you're friends with me?"

"No. She's not like that. It's just that she wants to be friends with those kids, and . . ."

"My friends and I are not as good as they are," Alicia finished my sentence for me.

It sounded so ugly when she said it.

"Alicia, I think you're great. And I bet Charlie does, too. We always agree on friends . . . or, at least, we used to. Just let me talk to her . . ."

Before I could finish, the bus pulled up and its doors whooshed open.

"I have to go, Sammie," she said quietly. "And you know what? I was wrong about you. I thought you were nice. I thought we could be friends. But I don't want to be friends with someone who doesn't think I'm good enough for her."

"Alicia, wait—"

"You'd better go," she said as the door shut. "Your *real* friends are waiting."

Alicia disappeared onto the bus, and as I turned around, I saw Lauren running up. She was waving a Starbucks card at me.

"I still have money left on my gift card," she said. "Come on. Frappuccino's on me."

I wasn't thirsty. In fact, I wanted to barf.

The Apology

....

Chapter 9

The next morning, I was waiting at the bus stop at seven thirty, but Alicia wasn't on the seven-thirty bus. She wasn't on the seven forty-five bus, either. I had hoped to catch her before school—to talk to her, to explain the truth behind what had happened. I had tried calling her the night before, but when her father, Candido, answered, he said she wasn't feeling well and had gone to bed. I figured she must have really been sick because Alicia wasn't on the eight o'clock bus, either.

In homeroom, I asked Sara if she had talked to Alicia.

"Yeah, we talked on the phone a lot last night," she said.

"About me?"

"About friends. You tell me, Sammie. Are you her friend?"

"I want to be."

"Then I have a suggestion for you," Sara said. "Try acting like one."

Wow. That was harsh. These Truth Tellers don't mess around.

I went through the day at school feeling lousy. You know how when you're mad at yourself, everything seems to go wrong? Well, that's how the whole day went. My bra strap broke after PE, and I had to hold it together with this huge, old safety pin which came undone in the middle of Spanish. I got back my history test, and I missed getting a B by half a point because I said the king of England during the American Revolution was George II. (Big deal, so it was George III. That's close enough for me.) And at lunch, Charlie talked to Jared the whole time and left me sitting at the table listening to Jillian's in-depth discussion of whether Ashley on *Real Teens* looked better as a blonde or a brunette. (Oh, and in case you're dying to know, brunette won.) Going into English, I dropped my backpack, which was unzipped, and all my pens fell out on the floor. Bernard of the drumsticks didn't even stop to help me pick them up. Sure, it was possible that he just didn't see them. But it was also possible that all the Truth Tellers were sticking up for Alicia and thought I deserved to get all my ballpoints trampled.

After school, Charlie was waiting for me at my locker.

"I'm not going home right away," I told her. "There's something I have to do."

"Dad's waiting for us. We have practice."

"I have to skip today."

"Sammie, we have a tournament this Sunday. Dad will freak out if you're not there."

"Can you cover for me, just this once?" I begged. "I'll let you borrow any of my clothes you want."

"I do that, anyway," she pointed out.

"Please, Charlie. This is important."

"Where are you going?"

"To Alicia's."

"You don't even know where she lives."

"I got her address from Sara. Tell Dad I'll be home by six. And I'll practice like a lunatic the rest of the week, I swear."

I think Charlie would have continued arguing with me, but just then, Lauren came up and asked her if she wanted to go to the gym with her to sign up for cheerleader tryouts.

"Of course I do," Charlie said, a big smile breaking across her face. "But afterward, I have to go to the club to practice."

"Perfect," Lauren answered. "We'll go sign up, and then I'll watch you work out. By the way, will Ryan be there? Not that it matters."

Right—*not that it matters.*

"Sure," Charlie said. "He lives there."

She picked up her backpack and slung it over her shoulder. "Okay, Sammie, I'm covering for you this time, but you'd better be there tomorrow," she whispered.

"I will be. Promise."

Charlie and Lauren started off down the hall, then, realizing they were leaving me behind, Lauren came back to talk to me.

"Listen, Sammie," she said, without the slightest bit of awkwardness. "I'd ask you to come, too, but I happen to know they're looking for girls who can fly, and I think you'd be kind of hard to lift."

She might as well have said "Sammie, you're a fat pig and harder to lift than a pregnant elephant." I felt like someone had punched me in the stomach, but luckily I was able to take in just enough air to spit out, "That's okay, Lauren. I have other plans, anyway."

Sara had given me directions to Alicia's house. She lived in a neighborhood called Palms, which wasn't too far from where we used to live in Culver City. I got on the bus and rode down Lincoln Boulevard until we reached Venice Boulevard, then transferred. There were no other kids on the bus, certainly no one from Beachside. It was a long way, and I had to admire Alicia for making the trip twice every day. I looked out the window, checking the street signs. The directions said to get off and walk a half block to Alicia's house, which was number 4307.

When I got off, I went into the little grocery store on the corner of Southwest and Venice and bought two pieces of red licorice, one for Alicia and one for me. Then I ate them both. Being nervous makes me eat. Actually, being anything makes me eat.

I headed down the block until I reached number 4307. I have to confess that I was a little surprised to see that Alicia's house was not a house, but an apartment. The building was three floors high, and there must have been seven or eight apartments on each floor. I never assumed it was an apartment because Sara hadn't given me an apartment number. So I just stood in front of the row of mailboxes searching for the name Bermudez. I was concentrating so hard that I didn't see Alicia come down the stairs and stand in back of me.

"Sammie, what are you doing here?" she said.

I nearly jumped ten feet in the air. I wheeled around to face her. I think you could safely say that she didn't look happy to see me. And that's an understatement.

"Oh, you scared me, Alicia."

"Why are you scared, Sammie? Because you've come to my part of town? It's not scary here, although I realize it's not the Sporty Forty."

"Alicia, I need to talk to you. You've got me all wrong."

"Do I? Is that why you wouldn't tell all those kids from the club that we're friends?"

"Can we go into your house, please?" I asked her. A bunch of little kids from the apartment building had gathered around and were looking at us curiously.

"Whatever."

She turned and headed up a flight of stairs and down an outside hallway to apartment 206. She pushed open the door, and as we went inside, my mouth started to water. It smelled completely delicious in there. An older woman was taking a pan out of the oven, and I realized that whatever smelled so great was in it.

"This is my grandmother, Anna Bermudez," Alicia said. *"Abuela, ésta es mi amiga Sammie."*

"Hola, Sammie," Mrs. Bermudez said to me. *"¿Quieres un tamal?"*

"She wants to know if you want one of her tamales," Alicia said. "I warn you, they're so good, you won't stop at one."

Alicia's grandma put a tamale on a plate for each of us, and we went outside and sat on the steps to eat them.

"I thought you were sick," I began, after I had

lapped up the last bite.

"I have a sore throat. I may be catching a cold. I didn't sleep much last night."

"Because of me? Oh, Alicia, I'm so sorry."

"Do you know how it feels, Sammie? To feel like I'm not good enough to be considered your friend? To be treated like I'm an embarrassment? Well, I'll tell you. It hurts."

"I know what it feels like, Alicia, because I feel that way, too. You think I'm comfortable with those Sporty Forty kids? I'm not. Lauren got interested in Charlie and me because she's in love with our brother. Now all of them like Charlie because she's working so hard at being one of them. But they don't really accept me. They just kind of put up with me."

"Then why do you hang out with them?"

"Because all my life, my sister and I have had the same friends. Charlie and I, we're like two halves of a circle. I wouldn't know what to do without her."

"I don't have a sister," Alicia said softly. "So I don't know what that feels like."

"Well, it feels wonderful," I explained. "I've never been lonely, not for one minute, because whenever I needed a best friend, Charlie was there."

"So that's why you're trying so hard to fit in? So hard that you couldn't even tell them about me?"

"I was wrong to do that, and I'm so sorry."

Alicia looked at me and her pretty brown eyes filled with tears.

"Besides," I continued, "it had nothing to do with you personally. Charlie really likes you. It's just all the others she didn't want them to know about. Not yet, anyway."

"The others? You mean the Truth Tellers?"

I nodded.

"Because we're different, right? Too weird for them?"

"Charlie wouldn't think that if she saw what goes on there. I know she wouldn't. She's got an open mind. Maybe I can even get her to come sometime. Then she'll see how cool everyone is."

Alicia looked surprised. "You mean you want to come back to Truth Tellers?"

"Yes, I really do. I haven't stopped thinking about it. When I was there, I felt so . . . fantabulous."

Alicia laughed. "You really do like that word, don't you?"

Then she reached out and gave me a hug.

Before I knew it, we were inside and Alicia was showing me the room that she shared with her little brother, Ramon. He was sitting on the floor with her grandmother, building a tower of blocks and then knocking it down. Each time the blocks fell, he screamed, "BOOM!" and laughed, flashing the most adorable dimples you've ever seen. Alicia showed me her collection of shirts that her grandmother embroidered with colorful flowers. We put on some music and danced, and pretty soon, both Ramon and

Alicia's grandmother had joined in. Her grandmother reminded me of GoGo—they both had the kind of smile that makes everyone else in the room smile, too.

We were having such fun that we didn't even notice when Candido came in. He looked surprised to see me.

"Sammie," he said. "Does your papa know you're here?"

My dad! I had almost forgotten. I checked the time and it was five thirty. I had promised Charlie I'd be home by six, and I was going to be really late if I took the bus. Since Candido had to go pick up Esperanza, he offered to drive me home. With a hug for Alicia, a hug for her grandmother, and a hug for Ramon (a careful one, since he was covered with mushed-up tamale, which didn't exactly make him a hug magnet), I left the apartment and climbed into Candido's truck.

"Your papa, he wasn't happy with you this afternoon," Candido said as his truck rattled down Venice Boulevard to the beach.

"Yeah, I was a no-show at practice."

"Charlie told him you had some kind of emergency."

"It was kind of an emergency," I said. When he looked at me funny, I explained. "Alicia and I had a fight. But we worked it out."

"So now you are friends?" he asked.

"Now we are friends," I answered. And I don't mind telling you, that sentence made me feel really great.

I got home five minutes after six, and my dad didn't lose one second starting in on the lecture about how no champion ever reached her full potential without hard work and dedication. Luckily, just when he was getting to the part about how anything good is worth working for, my mom called. My dad went into the kitchen to talk to her, and the lecture got cut short.

"Saved by the bell," Ryan said. "If I were you, Sam-I-Am, I'd make like a tree and leave."

I was in such a good mood that I actually laughed, even though he's been making that same joke since he was seven, and it wasn't even funny then. I ran to our room and pushed open the door. I couldn't wait to tell Charlie about my visit with Alicia and to invite her to come to Truth Tellers. But before I could get a word out, Charlie pounced on me, grabbed me by the hands, and twirled me around.

"You're not going to believe it!" she screamed. "The best news ever! I mean *ever*. Take a guess."

"Uh . . . Justin Bieber called and is coming here for dinner."

"Better!" She laughed.

"Okay. Justin Bieber is coming for dinner and he's bringing Zac Efron."

"Even better than that!"

"I give up, Charlie. There's nothing better than that."

"Oh, yes there is. Lauren called. And we're both invited to a makeover party at her house this Friday night!"

She grabbed my hands, squealed like a wild boar I saw once on the Discovery Channel, and twirled me around again.

"Tell me, Sam, if that isn't the coolest thing ever?"

She was so happy that there was no way I was going to tell her that I would have *much* preferred Justin Bieber stopping in for dinner.

"Girls, your mom wants to say hi," Dad said, sticking his head in our room. "Who wants to go first?"

"Sammie, let me tell her the news, okay?" Charlie said. She grabbed the phone and bolted into the hall, chattering so fast, even I could only barely understand what she was saying. I turned and caught a glimpse of myself in the mirror. OMG! Why hadn't anyone told me? My T-shirt was covered with liquidy blobs of mushed-up tamale. It looked like Ramon had wiped his face on me. *Nice work, Ramon.*

I burst out laughing.

Well, maybe the party invitation was a really good thing. I could certainly use a makeover, that was for sure.

The Makeover

....

Chapter 10

"Come on, Sammie. We're late. I promised Lauren we'd pick up the pizza before everyone gets there."

It was Friday evening, and I was rushing around, looking for a little bag of makeup that GoGo had given me. It was a purse-size, patent-leather bag she got for free from the makeup counter at Macy's, and it had samples of different colored lip glosses and eye shadows in it. She had given one to Charlie, too, but Charlie had already opened hers since she decided to start wearing makeup to school. I'd rather sleep the extra ten minutes in the morning than have to get up early to put on makeup, which just comes off in PE, anyway.

We were heading over to Lauren Wadsworth's house for the makeover party. All week, she had been telling Charlie how it was the SF2 girls' favorite party. Everyone started with a mani-pedi, and then each girl would give a makeover to another girl. Everyone brought all different kinds of makeup and hair accessories so they could experiment with new stuff. At the end of the evening, everyone went to get frozen yogurt looking totally glammed out.

Alicia and I had talked on the phone every night during the week and had been spending some time together in school, too. One day at lunch, I even left the SF2 table and ate with her. Her grandmother had sent a Tupperware container with two tamales in it and told Alicia one of them was for me. That afternoon, I asked Charlie to ask Lauren if I could bring Alicia to the makeover party. I thought if we all could hang out together, they'd see how great Alicia was and she'd get to see their good sides, too. But Lauren told Charlie I couldn't bring her, because there were already six of us, and her mom was paying for us to get mani-pedis and one more person would be too expensive. That made sense.

As I searched every drawer in my dresser, I could hear my dad honking the horn outside. He was driving us to Lauren's and picking us up at ten sharp to make sure we got to bed on time. Charlie and I were playing in another big qualifying tournament at the Sand and Surf Tennis Club that Sunday, and he wanted us to practice all day Saturday and be well rested for the tournament.

"You can't have a winning mind-set if you're tired," he reminded us.

Thank you, Dad. Oh, and by the way, what exactly is a winning mind-set? Is it anything like a Vulcan mind meld? I saw one of those on TV once.

My dad gave another impatient blast on the horn, and I decided I had to give up looking for GoGo's sample makeup bag. Just as I grabbed my purse and headed out, I found it. Guess where? No, you'll never guess. It was in Ryan's hand, which was behind his back. He was lurking in the corner of my room and had been there the whole time I was frantically searching.

"Looking for something?" He smirked.

"Ryan, you turkey leg! You had it all along, didn't you?"

"Come and get it," he said, holding the bag high above his head. "Let's see if Sammie can jump."

The truth is, I can jump, and I did. I ran up to him, sprang probably a foot in the air, and snatched the bag from his idiot hand.

"Whoa, you should give up tennis and go out for volleyball," he said. "Nice elevation."

"See you later, Ryan."

"Yes, you actually will. Lauren asked if I wanted to meet all you glamour-pusses for yogurt after the makeup bash. I'm bringing two friends. They're dying to meet the gorgeous Brooke."

"Forget it. She's dating the General."

"Maybe you didn't hear me, Sam-I-Am. I am bringing two *eighth*-graders. They're practically grown-ups."

"Oh, like you? Half the time you act like you're in kindergarten."

"So not true," he answered, sticking his tongue out and wrinkling his nose at me.

Yeah, I rest my case.

The honking horn reminded me there wasn't time to continue this conversation, so I shut up and hurried out to the car where Charlie was fuming. She had started to go nuts if we were ever late for anything with Lauren. It was like she was afraid that if she kept Lauren waiting, Lauren would change her mind and disinvite her. We were new to the SF2 group, and it wasn't like we were so "in" that we couldn't suddenly be "out."

We stopped at Barone's and picked up the two vegetarian pizzas we had ordered. Well, actually, we had asked Dad to order sausage and mushroom, but he said a certain someone didn't need to be eating fatty sausages. Duh, I wonder who he meant. The vegetarian pizzas were okay with Charlie, though, because she said the other girls would probably prefer vegetarian. Everybody was watching their weight.

So I assume those buttery, garlic rolls are out of the question? I'm sorry. Forget I even thought about the word buttery. *Or* roll.

You would not believe Lauren's house. It was at the top of a canyon a few blocks from the beach, with a view out over the Pacific Ocean all the way to Catalina Island. There was a circular driveway in front, with three very shiny, black cars parked in it—one SUV, one convertible, and one fancy sedan with blacked-out windows. In the middle of the driveway was a fountain, which had a stone cherub boy peeing up into the air and big goldfish swimming around in the pond below. Call me crazy, but if I had a stone fountain in front of my fancy house, I would have something different in the middle, like an angel or a bunch of lilies, or maybe even dancing ladies. I mean, who wants to look at a boy peeing every time you come home? I think we can all agree that's not the first thing you want to see.

Charlie and I rang the doorbell, and the most adorable little girl opened the door. She had curly, blond hair and big eyes that were so dark blue, they almost looked purple. She must have been three or four years old. At first she was smiling, but when she looked us up and down, she burst into tears.

"There's two of them!" she screamed, crying at the top of her little lungs. "Mommy, help! They're scary!"

Within a second, Lauren's mother appeared at the door. I recognized her from the club: She was tan and slender and always wore pearls. The little girl clutched her mommy's leg and hid her face so she couldn't see us.

"It's okay, Amanda," Mrs. Wadsworth said, picking her up. "They're twins. That's why they look so much alike." She took Amanda's hand and reached it out so that she touched our faces. "See, honey? It's two different girls who just look very, very much alike."

"I hate them," Amanda whined, jerking her hand back from our faces like she was touching a poisonous rattlesnake.

Mrs. Wadsworth shrugged, then smiled at us.

"She's never seen identical twins before," she whispered. "It'll take her a little time to get used to the idea. Then she'll be fine."

All the other girls had gathered in the entryway and were watching this humiliating scene unfold. There we were, Charlie and I, standing with two leaky, grease-stained pizza boxes, our dad's beat-up Toyota rumbling in the driveway, while the little stone boy shot pee five feet up into the air and the little beautiful girl sobbed at the very sight of us. Let me put it like this: It wasn't the best way to kick off the evening.

"Don't mind Amanda," Lauren said, showing us into the house. "She cries at everything scary."

Wow, I didn't know we were scary. We should charge admission. Step right up, folks, and for only two dollars, you can get a glimpse of those terrifying Diamond twins.

The inside of the house was huge, with pink marble floors and a crystal chandelier and large paintings of green and orange triangles on the walls. Not to be rude, but it looked like the Los Angeles County Museum of Art, which I've visited several times with GoGo. I was half expecting to see a uniformed guard strolling around, telling us not to touch the furniture.

We went into the kitchen where, to my total shock, I ran into Esperanza, Alicia's mother. At first, I was thrilled. I thought maybe Lauren had changed her mind and Alicia was coming to the party and Esperanza was just dropping her off. But then I realized that Esperanza was working.

"Esperanza works for you?" I whispered to Lauren.

"Just on Fridays when the regular housekeeper is off," she said.

Esperanza took the pizza boxes from my hands, set them on the table, and then got busy putting out plastic plates and paper napkins.

"Thank you, Esperanza," Mrs. Wadsworth said. "Just finish loading the dishwasher, and I'll have Mr. Wadsworth drive you to the bus stop, unless Candido is coming to pick you up."

I was so uncomfortable, I wanted to shrivel up and melt away. The last thing I wanted was to have Alicia's mother *waiting* on me.

"Hi, Esperanza," I said to her as the other girls

grabbed slices of pizza and headed over to the stairs. "It's so nice to see you."

That was lame. It's nice to see you cleaning up the kitchen after me? What am I saying?

"My Alicia, she likes you, Sammie," Esperanza answered. And then she whispered, "Not so much these other girls."

"Sammie, grab a slice so we can get started," Lauren called out. "We're doing our makeovers in my mom's bathroom because it's loaded with mirrors."

I turned to Esperanza. "Could you do me a big favor?" I asked her. "Don't tell Alicia you saw me here. I don't want her to feel bad."

Then, without waiting for her answer, I turned and ran toward the stairs.

"I thought we were going to do the mani-pedis first," I said.

"We are. We're doing them upstairs, too."

"But I thought your mom was paying for someone to come and do them here. Like a professional person."

"Where'd you get that idea?" Lauren asked.

While everyone headed up the stairs, I wedged my way over to Charlie. She didn't look up, just stared down at her paper plate like she'd never seen a slice of pizza before.

"You made up that whole mani-pedi thing, didn't you, Charlie? So you wouldn't have to invite Alicia?"

"I'm sorry, Sammie," she whispered back. "I didn't have the nerve to ask Lauren. I will next time, I promise."

I was so angry; I could feel my whole neck and face turn hot and red. She had lied to me. And for what? So she didn't have to feel embarrassed about asking if Alicia could come? She could have just told me, and then I would have asked Lauren myself.

Or would I have? Maybe I would have chickened out, too. Besides, what if Alicia had come and then had to watch her mother setting the table for us and loading the dishwasher? That would have been horrible. This was all so confusing. Maybe Charlie had done the right thing after all.

Lauren's mom's bathroom was the size of our bedroom. I'm not kidding. Two people could sleep in there—not that anybody really wants to sleep in a bathroom, but you get the picture. There were mirrors on all four walls and a shower that had six jets coming out of the sides, plus a huge, round showerhead above. If you took a shower in there, you didn't even have to scrub—you could just stand there like a car going through a car wash.

We sat down on the floor, and everyone put the makeup they had brought in the middle of our circle. Jillian brought the most stuff: rhinestone bobby pins, about twelve pots of lip gloss in all different colors and flavors, a bunch of different shades of purple nail polish, makeup brushes in every size, and tons of long, dangly earrings with different sparkling stones. She said she had seen on *Teen Beauty Secrets* that dangly things were in this season. The stuff Lily brought was great and so creative: necklaces with colored beads that she had collected in thrift stores, scarves to tie up our hair that she had made from old dresses she had outgrown, and black eyeliner for creating what she called a "Goth evening look." Brooke's mother gave her all of her old blushes, and she had an entire shoe box full of them.

"My mom's really pale." Brooke laughed as she dumped about thirty blushes onto the floor.

Lauren's mother supplied the rest: headbands, eye shadows by the handful, eyebrow pencils, bronzers, lip liners, little bottles of lotions that smelled like peaches and roses and lavender, and body powder that sparkled gold when you puffed it on.

"Let's hold hands in a circle for a minute," Jillian said, "and say how grateful we are to have all this makeup to put on."

"That is so corny," Brooke said.

"No, it's not," Jillian answered. "I saw them do it on *Real Teen Makeovers*. It made me cry. I loved, loved, loved the circle."

"I think it's a nice idea," I said. "I've been in something called an acceptance circle. Everyone in the circle agrees to accept one another just the way they are. It's extremely cool."

"And extremely weird," Lauren said.

I looked over at Charlie and knew she wanted me to drop the subject. So I did. I didn't really want to discuss the acceptance circle with these girls, anyway.

There were six of us there, so we divided up into makeover teams of two. Lauren and Charlie were one team. No surprise there. They were practically in love these days. I wanted to team up with Lily because I thought she had the best style and would create a look for me that I liked. But she picked Brooke because she wanted to give her a "soldier look", so she'd go even better with the General. That left me with Jillian. Everyone said we went well together because we were both into circles. And I don't think they meant that in a nice way.

We spent the next hour decorating ourselves. Jillian painted my fingernails and toenails a purple so dark, it looked almost black. When she did my makeup, she put it on and took it off at least a million times. She tried green eye shadow and thought it didn't do anything for my brown eyes. She dabbed on purple, but thought it made me look like a vampire. She thought gold was too slutty, gray was too ladylike, blue was too bright, ivory was too pale, magenta was too flashy, silver was too glowy ... I have never heard anyone with so many opinions about eye shadow. By the time she settled on copper, my eyelids were so sore, I was begging her to move on to lip gloss.

But she did the same thing with lip gloss. Cherry red made my teeth look yellow. Plum was too dull. Coral was too nothing. Blazing Pink was too babyish. Radiance was too shimmery. Natural was too plain.

I can't even describe what happened when she

got to the blush question. Let me just say that by the time she had tried at least ten colors of blush, my cheeks were bright red from her rubbing them with the Kleenex. The last thing I needed was more color in my cheeks. What I needed was medical attention!

For the whole hour, no one talked about anything but makeup. Now, don't get me wrong, I enjoy a good makeup conversation, but by the end of the hour, my mind rebelled. It was on makeup conversation overload.

"Does this smoky-gray eyeliner make my eyes pop?" Brooke asked.

Why would you want your eyes to pop? I thought. *That would be so totally messy and gooey.*

"If you put blush on the end of your nose, will it make it look shorter?" Lauren wondered.

Who knows? I thought. *Why don't you ask Pinocchio?*

"Do you think this soldier look is too overboard?" Lily asked, stepping back to examine Brooke's eyes.

Yes, she looks like Count Dracula himself.

"Will mascara run if you cry?" Charlie asked Lauren.

Beats me, my darling sister. But I'll tell you this: I want to run away from here right now.

By the time we finished, I was so bored with the makeover talk that I couldn't wait to leave. Unlike Truth Tellers, which just whizzed by, this was the longest hour of my life. And to top it off, I didn't even look that good. The eyeliner made my eyes itch and I just wanted to rub them. Jillian had combed my hair into this sophisticated updo that succeeded in making my face look really fat. My almost-black fingernails and toenails looked like I had developed some sort of fungus rot. And I think we've discussed the red, irritated cheek look, which wasn't all that flattering.

All the other girls looked very glamorous. Lauren couldn't look bad if she tried, and neither could Brooke. Lily had this modified Goth look that was unique and quirky. Jillian had taken over from me when I pooped out on new makeup ideas and made herself into a flashy, glittery starlet, which thrilled her to no end and suited her, too. And my sister, Charlie, looked great—with a velvet headband and pale-blue eye shadow and eyeliner that actually did make her eyes pop, not in that squirty way, but in a very nice way.

As we piled into Lauren's mom's SUV and drove to meet up with the guys at Chilly's Frozen Yogurt in the mall, I wondered why I was the only makeover failure. Was I just pathetic or what? Where was that person who had felt so free and comfortable at Truth Tellers and with Alicia? The one who felt so fantabulous in her own skin?

And then it occurred to me. That girl didn't need a makeover. She was already fantabulous just the way she was.

She was the real me.

Ranked

....

Chapter 11

"Hit it to the fat one. She's got lead in her feet," I heard the girl in the blue tennis skirt whisper to her partner. I wasn't supposed to hear it, but I did.

It was late Sunday morning. Charlie and I had recovered from the makeover party and spent the whole day before hitting tennis balls with our dad. According to him, we were ready, in shape, and primed to start our first match of the day at the Sand and Surf Tennis Club qualifying tournament. If we won, we'd earn our ranking. We had just met our competition, two girls from the Malibu Racquet Club. One was Kimberly McCall, and the one in the blue skirt calling me fat was Nicole Dennis. We had played them before, and they were tough competitors.

Charlie heard Nicole say it, too, and saw my

face turn beet red with anger.

"You have to put it out of your mind," she warned me.

That was easy for Charlie to say, weighing 105 pounds. She didn't understand that when you're overweight, every fat insult stays in your memory forever.

"I can't," I whispered to Charlie. "She makes me so mad."

"Good," she answered. "Then use it. Show her you're not slow. Make her eat those words."

Charlie and I won the racket spin, which meant we got to serve first. Our usual strategy is to have Charlie serve the first game because she's got a killer serve. But this time she said to me, "You serve first, Sam. Show her your stuff."

I looked up in the stands and caught sight of our family. They were hard to miss because GoGo was wearing her floppy, purple hat with a big, flashy, silver pin on the front. When she made that pin, she said the design was a combination of *S* and *C*, our first initials. She always wears it for our special occasions—I have pictures in my scrapbook of her wearing it at my kindergarten graduation. I was crying because I didn't want to leave Ms. Updegrove, the best kindergarten teacher in the world.

When GoGo saw me looking up in the stands, she put both her hands in the air and gave us a double thumbs-up. My dad was sitting next to her with his face straight ahead, staring intensely at us. He does that on purpose when we play, his dark-brown eyes boring into us like lasers. He calls it the Super Focus Look, and he actually believes he is beaming us the motivation to concentrate. It was working today, because I was feeling all of my powers focused on beating Nicole Dennis. I wasn't going to let her call me fat and get away with it.

I was so focused, in fact, that it didn't even bother me that Lauren was there. Ryan had invited her, and she was sitting next to him. I did notice that they were holding hands, in front of my dad and everything! I guess that made it official. They were doing the boyfriend-girlfriend thing, which did not make me happy.

Not now, Sammie. Focus. Nicole Dennis called you fat. You have to beat her bony little butt.

It's totally amazing what the desire to get revenge can do to your tennis serve. My first serve to Nicole was so good, I could actually hear a murmur from the crowd in the stands. And the second one, which I directed right to her backhand, zoomed by her so fast, she didn't even get her racket on it. I could see her looking over at Kimberly with a *what-the-heck-has-gotten-into-this-girl?* look.

Macaroni and cheese. That's what's gotten into this girl. Power fuel.

They didn't score a point the first game. Or the second or the third. I played like my feet were on fire, springing, pouncing, lunging like a tiger chasing an antelope . . . or whatever it is tigers chase. I could hear Ryan cheering for me in the stands.

"You go, Sam-I-Am!" he called, standing up to do an in-place robot move. "You're blazing!"

From the corner of my eye, I could see my dad pull Ryan back down to a sitting position. Tennis competitions are kind of old-school, and you're not really supposed to scream and yell, and for sure there is no robot dancing allowed in the stands. As usual, Ryan couldn't have cared less about the rules.

"Wow," Charlie said to me after we won the first set six games to one. "Where have you been all summer?"

"In hibernation," I said. "But the bear is back. Hear me growl."

And then I roared. You heard me. I roared like an actual grizzly bear. I hoped Nicole Dennis heard that.

I heard another roar from up in the stands. I looked up and saw Ryan standing on his seat, pounding his chest, and roaring back at me. Then I saw Lauren pull him back down into his seat. She looked embarrassed. Obviously, roaring in public was not high on the Sporty Forty list of acceptable things to do.

It felt good to be playing so great. The truth is, I hadn't been fired up about tennis for months. Maybe it was because I had gained the extra weight; it's hard to run your butt off when you can feel it jiggling behind you. Or maybe it was because our dad is so intense about tennis that it makes it hard to pursue other activities. The more I got interested in new things, the more I had been drifting away from tennis. But I can tell you this: Nicole "The Mouth" Dennis had certainly gotten my attention back on the game. I hadn't played like that in forever.

We beat Kimberly and Nicole in straight sets, six-one, and six-love. When they came to the net to shake hands after the match, I smiled at Nicole.

"Fat girl makes good," I said.

"You just had a lucky day," she answered. "And by the way, you could still lose a few pounds."

My dad practically flew down to the court to congratulate us.

"You did it, girls!" His smile was so big, you could probably see all thirty-two of his teeth. "Charlie, you were incredible at the net. And, Sammie, wow. You reached into your inner tennis player and pulled out championship-quality moves."

"I'm so proud of you both," GoGo added, handing us some blue Gatorade, which I needed because I was oozing my usual twenty gallons of sweat.

"Yeah, you chickadees owned the court!" Ryan said. "Diamonds rule, don't they, Lauren?"

Lauren nodded and threw her arms around Charlie to give her a hug. Then she went to hug me, but after looking me up and down, hesitated.

"That's okay," I said. "I'm pretty damp. I wouldn't want to hug me, either."

We gathered our things and walked off the court together. At the clubhouse, we had to stop to fill out a bunch of forms that put us officially on the circuit for ranked players. Now the tournaments we'd play in would be with only the best Under-14 players, and after each tournament, our ranking would go up or down depending on how we did.

"So, girls," my dad said as we headed to the parking lot. "Now that you've got your ranking, the next goal is to make it into the top ten. They call it the Top Ten Club, and trust me, it's where you want to be."

"Rick, for goodness' sake," GoGo said. "They just got into *this* club, now you want them in the *next* one. Give them a minute to enjoy it."

"You don't get ahead by resting on your laurels, Phyllis. If they get ranked in the top ten in the state, college scholarships are going to come pouring in."

College scholarships! Gee, Dad, how about if I just pass Algebra I first?

"We start tomorrow, girls. School's over at three. Home by three thirty. Grab a high-protein, low-fat snack, and we're on the courts at three forty-five."

Oops. Not so fast.

The next day was Monday. I had promised Alicia I'd go to Truth Tellers. Even more important, I had promised *myself* I'd go to Truth Tellers.

"Uh, Dad? I can't make it tomorrow," I said quietly.

"Excuse me?" he said. "I must have misheard you

because it sounded like you said that you can't make it tomorrow."

"I did say that."

"Oh boy," Ryan commented to Lauren. "This isn't going to be pretty."

"There's something I have to do after school," I continued. "A new activity."

"What activity could possibly be more important than tennis practice?" My dad's voice crackled with irritation.

I looked at Charlie and Lauren. Did I dare say the truth? Charlie knew that I had gone to Truth Tellers, but I know she hadn't mentioned it to Lauren. Would she die of embarrassment if I told everyone? And what about Lauren—would she think I was the biggest geek in the world? I could lie and say I had to go to study hall to catch up on math homework.

Wait just a minute, Sammie girl. You're going to Truth Tellers and you're actually considering not telling the truth? Yeah, that makes a whole lot of sense.

Okay, I thought. *I'm going to take a risk. Let's see what the truth feels like.*

"Well, now that you asked, Dad," I plunged in, "I'm joining a club at school that meets every Monday. It's called Truth Tellers, and it's really cool. We do monologues and public speaking and tell the truth about our feelings."

He stared at me like I had suddenly started

speaking in Swahili or Greek or Mongolian or some other foreign language.

"And this activity will help your tennis game how?" he asked.

"Actually, it has nothing to do with tennis, Dad. It's just something I'm interested in and makes me feel good."

He stared at me with that laser look. I felt like his eyes were burning a hole in my forehead. It was Lauren who broke the silence.

"Ewww, Sammie," she said. "Don't you mind hanging around with all those weird kids?"

Thank you, Lauren, for adding your two cents, which, if you ask me, weren't even worth that much.

"They're not so weird, Lauren, once you get to know them." I looked over to Charlie for support. "Isn't that right, Charlie?"

She paused and I could tell she didn't know what to say. I had put her in a tough position. Finally, she managed to say, "Well, Alicia's pretty nice."

"You mean whatshisname's daughter?" Lauren asked. "The cleanup guy?"

That did it for me. "His name is Candido," I snarled. "And Alicia is practically my best friend."

"Since when?" Charlie asked, clearly surprised.

"Since *you* seem to have found a new best friend," I snapped back at her.

"That's not the way I see it, Sammie."

"Then maybe you should get glasses, Charlie."

"Girls, girls," GoGo said, putting her arms around both Charlie and me. "You're both tense from the match. Now I say you sit down together and talk this out, just like you always do. I think you're due for a Pizza Bonding session, if I'm not mistaken."

"Pizza Bonding?" Lauren said. "Sounds fun."

"It's something the girls have done for many years after every match," GoGo explained. "There's nothing like a good talk and a cheesy pizza, that's what I believe." Then, in a voice that sounded a little firmer than usual, she added, "It's always just the two of them. Right, girls?"

I was half expecting Charlie to ask if Lauren could come, but she didn't. She knew that would have seriously hurt my feelings.

Lauren left with Ryan. They were going to walk down the beach to the Sporty Forty. It was a long walk, about two miles, but I figured it would give them lots of time to hold hands. GoGo took us back to the club where we called our mom, took showers, and changed. Then she dropped us off at Barone's.

"Talk it out, girls," she told us as we climbed out of the car. "That's what sisters do."

As we sat at our usual booth at Barone's munching on our sausage and mushroom pizza, Charlie and I actually did have a good talk about what had happened. I told her I didn't like Lauren criticizing my friends and looking down on Alicia.

"I know those kids seem different," I explained to her, "but they're so much fun. I think you'd really like them if you gave them half a chance."

"And I think you'd really like the SF2s if you weren't so busy judging them all the time."

"I don't know. Those girls worry so much about how they look," I commented.

"Sammie, this may come as a shock to you, but there is nothing wrong with looking good."

She had a point. But so did I. In the end, we decided that sometime in the future, Charlie would stop in and visit Truth Tellers. And I would at least attempt to wear mascara to school. We raised our glasses of vanilla Coke.

"To us," I said.

"Always and forever," she said.

We clinked glasses and both felt much better. I wish it could have stayed that way, but it didn't.

Caught in the Act

....

Chapter 12

"Our topic for today is 'out of place,'" Ms. Carew said as the members of Truth Tellers gathered in our acceptance circle the next day.

"My hair's out of place," Sara said. "Has been ever since I was born."

Everyone cracked up, including me. I had finally convinced my dad to let us skip tennis practice that Monday so I could attend Truth Tellers. It worked out for Charlie, too, because she could go to cheerleading with Lauren. They had to learn the routines for tryouts, and the cheerleading coach was holding classes on Monday afternoons.

In English that day, I had told Ms. Carew that I was joining Truth Tellers for sure.

"That's fantabulous, Sammie," she had said.

There is that word again. I haven't heard it once for twelve and three-quarters years, and suddenly it seems to pop up every other day.

"I know what you mean about unruly hair," Ms. Carew was saying to Sara, "but today we're talking about a different meaning of 'out of place.' Today, I want us to work on revealing a time we *felt* out of place, a time when we didn't belong."

"No problem!" Etta said. "I feel that way every day. You try having green hair in a school full of blondes."

"Or having black skin," Devon added.

"Or brown," Alicia agreed. Everyone nodded.

"If there's one thing middle schoolers know about, it's feeling out of place," Ms. Carew said. "This is a time when you're all trying to find where you belong, and that's not easy."

I couldn't believe it. We had only been discussing the topic for thirty seconds, and already my mind was spinning with ideas. All the times I had felt out of place: in kindergarten, when I was the only one who just couldn't get how to use scissors. In gymnastics, when every other girl could touch her toes and I couldn't get past my knees. And just the other night, at the makeover party, when everyone but me looked great in gold, sparkly eye shadow.

"The reason I want us to work on this topic," Ms. Carew continued, "involves some very exciting news. The Santa Monica City Council has asked to hear from local young people about their experiences living in our community. Principal Pfeiffer asked if our group could represent Beachside Middle School with one of our performances. He suggested we select a topic of interest to middle schoolers. I thought if we presented 'Feeling Out of Place,' it would give everyone a chance to speak from the heart."

"Wow, you mean we'll perform at a real, actual city council meeting?" Bernard asked.

"More than that," Ms. Carew answered. "We won't just be speaking to the city council. We'll be doing our performance at a community-wide meeting they're holding in the Civic Auditorium."

"No way," Alicia said. "I went to a Christmas show there once. That place is huge."

"About three thousand seats, actually," Ms. Carew told us. "You guys would have quite an audience. It would give you a chance to make a real impact."

There were murmurs of "awesome" and "unbelievable" and "amazing" in the room.

"We're going to be famous," Etta said, high-fiving Devon.

"No one gets famous without doing the work first," Ms. Carew said. "So let's get started. Who wants to begin? Each of you should do a brief introduction, and then I want you to act out the scene. Show us how you experience feeling out of place. Make us understand."

Will Lee volunteered first.

"This year, my parents made me go to ballroom dancing classes. I was the youngest and shortest boy in my class, and they paired me up with the tallest girl. It went a little something like this."

Will got up from the circle and walked to the front of the room. Craning his neck like he was looking at a giraffe in the zoo, he said, "May I have this dance, Gina?" He waited a minute in total silence. Then he stood on his tiptoes and gave a little wave, trying to get the imaginary Gina's attention. "Yo! I'm down here, Gina. Yeah, that's me, next to your knees. No, I'm not a midget. I'm just short."

We all howled with laughter, not just because it was funny, but because we all knew what it felt like to be out of place at your first dance.

Alicia went next, and she blew me away with her performance.

"Last year, I decided I wanted to be a cheerleader," she began. "I practiced to learn all the routines, but at tryouts, I realized how out of place I was, how different from the other girls."

She walked to the front of the room and pretended like she was standing in front of the cheerleading coaches.

"My name is Alicia Bermudez, and I'm going to do a routine to the school fight song."

Then she did it, singing "Go, Beachside Bulldogs" and performing a perfect routine that ended with two spectacular cartwheels.

"Thank you," she said to the imaginary judges. "Thank you so much. Oh yes, I'd love to be on the squad. Great! I'm so happy. Oh . . . you have to *pay* for your own uniforms? How much do they cost? Oh, wow. That's a lot. Okay, I'll talk to my parents and let you know. No, I'm sure it won't be a problem."

Then, with tears in her eyes, she sat back down and spoke to us quietly. "My grandmother got sick and we had to pay for her doctor bills. It took every cent we had saved. I never asked my parents for the uniform money. I just told the coaches that I had changed my mind and decided that cheerleading wasn't for me after all."

Everyone applauded. I jumped up to give Alicia a hug, and then so did everyone else in the room. Ms. Carew had tears in her eyes.

"Telling the truth is powerful," she said. "Alicia, I hope you'll consider repeating what you just did at the Civic Auditorium."

I was the new kid in the group, and I still wasn't completely comfortable getting up in front of everyone. So I waited and watched. Bernard did a piece about how he felt on his first day of school after arriving from Russia without knowing a word of English. Keisha made me cry when she acted out how kids teased her when she had to wear this horrible head contraption for six months to fix her jaw before she got braces. Sara was hilarious showing how it feels to get your hair done when you have a giant head of frizzy curls and the style is to have perfectly straight hair. By the time each person had performed, I felt comfortable enough to volunteer. It was like being in a room with really good friends.

It wasn't hard for me to pick a situation to act out. I had one fresh in my mind, a night when I couldn't have felt more out of place: the makeover party.

I cleared my throat and began.

"Last week, I attended my first makeover party with a bunch of girls. They spent the whole hour getting beautiful, and I spent the whole hour feeling ugly. I have never felt so out of place in my life."

With that, I got up and walked to the front of the room. At first I was self-conscious as I pretended to be Lauren Wadsworth. "Okay, you guys," I said. "Everybody put your makeup in the center of the room. Are you ready to be beautiful, because I know I am!"

Several of the kids in the circle started to giggle. Their laughter encouraged me to let loose a little more.

"Pass me that strawberry lip gloss," I said, imitating Brooke. "I love, love, love strawberry. It's just so kissable." And I made a smooching sound with my lips.

The kids were laughing now

And then I imitated myself, standing around awkwardly, looking uncomfortable and pathetic.

"I'm just not the makeup type," I said in my own voice. "And for sure, I don't feel kissable."

"Come on, Sammie," I said, going back to my

Lauren voice. "Don't be a freak. Get a little glam going, girlfriend. Like me."

Then I put my hands on my hips and did this really flirty walk all around the room. Everyone was laughing and I was totally absorbed in the moment—focused, as my dad would say. But when I completed my walk and turned around to face the group, I suddenly stopped dead in my tracks. I hadn't noticed that the hall door was open and standing there in the doorway was my sister. And standing right next to her, with her mouth hanging open, was Lauren Wadsworth.

"How could you?" Charlie gasped. There were tears in her eyes. "I mean, Sammie, *how could you*?"

All I could do was stand there. I had no answer.

"I have to go," I said to the group and, without looking back for an instant, bolted from the room, chasing Charlie and Lauren down the hall.

"Charlie, wait up," I called.

She and Lauren kept walking. They didn't even turn around.

"Let me explain. Please."

Charlie whipped her head around, saying, "There is nothing to explain," and then continued down the corridor toward the front door.

I ran as fast as I could to catch up with them. I came up alongside Charlie just as she was reaching the front exit. I almost threw my body in front of her, but she and Lauren just stepped around me and left the building. It wasn't until they were almost at the bottom of the brick steps that I was able to get in front of them and stand there face-to-face with them, so there was no avoiding me.

"We had an assignment," I began. "To act out a time when we felt out of place. That's all I was doing. Honest."

"You had no right," Charlie said.

"That was *my* party for *my* friends in *my* house," Lauren said. "I don't want what we do broadcast all over the school, just because you and your dorky pals in there have some stupid assignment."

"It was about me. It wasn't about you."

"Really? Well, it sure sounded like me. And I don't remember giving you permission to talk about my private matters, let alone my lip gloss preferences."

"I'll go back and tell them it wasn't you," I begged as Lauren pushed past me. "I'll explain."

Charlie looked at me, tears running down her face now. "You know these girls are important to me, Sammie. They're my friends. We trust one another. And you have gone and ruined it all for me."

"I didn't mean to hurt anyone," I said to her.

"Well, you did," she said.

Deep inside, I knew she was right.

I tried to answer, but Charlie wouldn't let me talk. She pushed me aside and ran past the flagpole and onto the sidewalk to where Lauren was waiting.

Separate Ways

....

Chapter 13

"So I hear there were some major fireworks after school today," Ryan said at dinner that night as he chomped noisily on his steak. He could use some table manners.

Charlie and I were sitting across from each other, but we hadn't said a word since we got home. Every time I tried to talk to her, she'd put her earbuds in and turn up the volume on her iPod.

"Oh, did some of the students have an argument?" GoGo asked. "And, Ryan, please chew with your mouth closed. It looks like a meat grinder in there."

GoGo laughed at her little joke, but no one else did. Charlie and I just stared into our plates and didn't make eye contact with anyone.

"I hear our very own Sam-I-Am told a little too

much truth at Truth Tellers," Ryan said.

"Did Lauren tell you that?" I asked him.

"As a matter of fact, she did. In between the tears, that is."

"Honey, did you make Lauren cry?" GoGo asked me. "That's not like you."

"I was doing a scene for Truth Tellers," I said.

"I still don't see why you participate in that," Dad threw in.

"Because I like it, Dad. Anyway, I said something that Lauren didn't want me to say."

"Correction," Charlie interrupted. "She was talking about things that she had no business talking about."

"It's my life, too, Charlie. I happened to be talking to my friends about me."

"Well, next time, leave me and my friends out of it."

"Girls," my dad said. "I want this bickering to stop right now. You've each said what you have to say. Now shake hands like we do on the tennis court. Match over, no hard feelings."

I reached my hand out across the table, but Charlie didn't take it.

"Honestly, I didn't mean to embarrass you," I explained to her in what I thought was a really nice tone of voice. "I was just expressing my feelings."

"Well, do me a favor and don't. And while you're at it, you can stay away from my friends."

"No problem there," Ryan chimed in. "I don't think they're too hot on seeing her, anyway."

Okay, Sammie. You can put your hand down now before it falls totally asleep. It's not looking like a handshake is in your future.

"All friends go through difficult times," GoGo said, standing up to clear her plate. "Sisters, too. When you love someone, you apologize, forgive, and make up."

"Well, I'm not apologizing," Charlie said. "I didn't do anything wrong. She did."

"Charlie." My dad sighed. "How do you expect to work together with Sammie on the court if you can't forgive and forget?"

"I don't want to play with her," she answered.

"Well, that's not an option, because I've just gotten your schedule for the fall circuit. You two have a match every other weekend starting this Sunday. Two o'clock in the afternoon. Your first division-ranked match. You play Kozlov and Shin from the SoCal Racquet Club in San Diego."

"What if I won't play?" Charlie asked.

"As I just said, that is not an option."

"I've got a great idea!" Ryan grinned. "They can just stay mad at each other and instead of playing tennis, let them put on a huge, old hair-pulling contest. Like lady wrestlers. We could charge admission."

He sprang to his feet, came over to me, and yanked my ponytail.

"Owww!" I screamed.

"That's good, Sam-I-Am. See what I mean? People pay to see pain."

Before I could get out of my chair and chase him around the house, Dad's phone rang. It was our mom. Charlie begged for the phone and went into our room. As she left, I heard her talking in an angry whisper. I didn't have to guess what she was talking about. It's spelled *M-E*.

A few minutes later, she came out of our room and handed me the phone.

"She wants to talk to you," she said. "Oh, and she said to shake hands and make up. So here you go."

Charlie stuck out her hand in a pretty unfriendly manner. I shook it. It wasn't the most heartfelt handshake in the world, but it was a start.

"Thanks, Charlie," I said, trying to make up.

"I'm only doing it because she told me to."

Houston, we have a problem. Mission Kiss-and-Make-Up failed before takeoff.

I took the phone and went in our room.

"Charlie told me what happened," Mom began, "and I think you should apologize. It's so upsetting to think that you girls are fighting and I'm not there to help you work it out."

"I did apologize, Mom. She didn't accept it. But I'll do it again, if it makes you feel any better."

"Good," she said. "And one more thing, Sammie. I want you to know that I understand your point of view, too. You're reaching out for new interests and new friends. It's normal to want to experiment, to find out who you really are. That's what I'm doing all the way across the country in Boston. Just remember that your sister is doing the same thing. Be considerate and tolerant of each other."

"Okay, Mom."

"I love you, sweetie."

"Love you, too."

Then she hung up.

My throat was all tight and I got big tears in my eyes, not because my mom was *mad* at me, but because she *understood* me. Aside from GoGo, she was the only one who seemed to realize what being a part of Truth Tellers meant to me.

Things between Charlie and me were pretty chilly that night. Somehow, though, I half expected that when we woke up in the morning, the chill would have worn off and we'd be like we always were.

Um . . . not so much. In fact, things were not only chilly, they were flat-out arctic.

When I got out of bed, Charlie was gone. She had left me a note that said, "See you in school. Or not."

Wow, that note is so cold, I'm surprised it doesn't have icicles hanging from it.

I walked to school alone. When I got to the corner of Third and Arizona, I ran into Alicia as she was getting off the bus.

"Did you and Charlie make up last night?" she asked. "I wanted to call, but I had to babysit for Ramon. By the way, he sends you a big, old, mushy-tamale kiss."

I smiled. Boy, did that feel good. I hadn't smiled since yesterday afternoon. As we walked to our lockers, I told Alicia about how angry Charlie was. In the midst of my story, we ran into Ms. Carew in the corridor.

"Sammie, do you have a second to talk?" she asked.

"I'll meet you later," Alicia said, leaving me alone with Ms. Carew.

"I was concerned about you yesterday when you didn't come back to Truth Tellers," Ms. Carew began. "I could see that your sister was upset with you."

"That's the understatement of the year."

"I'll bet you're very close, aren't you? Twins usually are."

"Identical twins, especially," I added.

"You and Charlie are so much alike on the outside, but inside, you're very different individuals, Sammie. You do understand that, don't you?"

I did and I didn't. Up until now, I had always felt

like Charlie and I were more alike than different. Not identical, but *almost* identical. But this fight we were having was an indication of how truly different we were. Or, at least, how truly different we were *becoming*.

"You remember what the poet Maya Angelou said?" Ms. Carew asked.

I nodded. "'Success is liking yourself, liking what you do, and liking how you do it.'"

"That's right," Ms. Carew said. "You and Charlie each have to find your own ways to success. And that may take you down separate paths."

The homeroom bell rang, and we each had to get to class. As Ms. Carew was hurrying off, she turned to me and said, "I hope you stick with Truth Tellers. It's a good path for you."

And then she was gone, disappearing into the throng of kids rushing from their lockers to class.

I didn't run into Charlie all morning, but I figured we'd see each other at lunch. As I walked up to the pavilion, I saw her sitting at the SF2 table, talking and laughing with Spencer. I was relieved to see she didn't look angry in the least. I waved and started over there, but before I got to the table, she jumped up from the bench and came to meet me.

"Hey," I said. "I missed you this morning."

"I left early. I just think we need a little space, you know? We're not exactly on the same wavelength right now."

"Separate paths?" I said, quoting Ms. Carew.

She nodded. "That's a good way to say it."

Suddenly, she looked really uncomfortable, and then blurted out what was on her mind.

"So maybe it's best if you don't eat with us for a little while," she said. "Lauren's not too happy with you. And having you at our table makes me . . . I don't know . . . a little uncomfortable."

I was stunned.

"Are you saying you don't want me there?"

"Well . . . sort of. I mean, yes. I mean, just for a while. Until things calm down."

I'm going to cry. Right here in the middle of the Beachside Middle School lunch pavilion. I'm going to burst into tears and flood the whole place until it's totally underwater.

Charlie reached out and took my hand.

"Don't look so sad, Sammie. It's not like you don't have your own friends. See, they're all sitting over there, having a great old time. You can go be with them."

I looked around and noticed Alicia, Sara, Etta, and Bernard at their table in the sun, sharing food from their brown-bag lunches.

"Hey, Charlie," I heard Spencer call out. "Get back here. Your bench is getting cold."

"Coming," she hollered back. "I think he's really cute. Great abs, too." And without another word, she turned and took her place next to Spencer at the SF2 table. I went and sat with Alicia, but truthfully, I spent a whole lot of the time glancing over at Charlie's table. From the looks of it, I think I was missing her more than she was missing me.

All week in school, it felt so weird not to be hanging out with Charlie. I just couldn't adjust to the new rules. I mean, it wasn't like I never saw her. We still practiced tennis after school every day. We congratulated each other on good shots and discussed strategy at the dinner table. And we stopped snarling at each other. But at school, it was almost like we were strangers. She hung out with her friends, and I hung out with mine.

The strangest day of all was Friday. Dad had given us the day off practice to let our muscles recover for the next day's workout, which was going to be a doozy, he said. We had our first big match on Sunday, and he wanted us to be in tip-top shape. It was great to come home after school and not have to hit the courts. It was one of those hot September days like we often get at the end of summer, ninety degrees without even so much as a breeze. Dad was giving Mr. Hornblower his weekly tennis lesson, and I was sitting out on the beach, just watching the waves break, when my phone rang. It was Alicia calling to say that Ms. Carew had called a special meeting of Truth Tellers for that night. Anyone who could make it was supposed to meet at school in the multipurpose room.

"What's up?" I asked her. "Why the special meeting?"

"She said that due to a scheduling conflict, they had to change the date of the city council meeting. It's sooner than she expected. We have to have an emergency rehearsal so we can be ready."

"Cool," I said. "I'm not doing anything. Besides, I have a new idea for my performance piece that I want to try out."

"Good idea. The makeover party didn't work out so well for you."

"You think?"

Alicia chuckled. I was glad I could at least make a joke about it now.

"By the way, Sammie, do you think your dad can drive us tonight? Mine has to work."

"I'll ask him," I said. "But I'm sure it's okay. He's supposed to be giving an hour tennis lesson, but I don't think it will go that long. Poor Mr. Hornblower looks like he could use some serious hydration, and he's only been hitting for ten minutes."

"Great. I mean, not for poor Mr. Hornblower, but for us. Rehearsal's at six thirty."

"No problem. We'll get you at five thirty."

I wandered into the kitchen to tell GoGo the good news about the performance. I hoped she'd be able to make it. I really wanted my dad to come, too. When he saw me onstage at the Civic Auditorium, he'd have to understand my interest in Truth Tellers. I mean, when was the last time he performed in front of the city council?

GoGo wasn't in the kitchen, but she had said she was coming over after school, so I expected her any minute. I looked out the window toward Pacific Coast Highway and saw her car making the left turn into our driveway. I ran outside to meet her.

"Just in time to help me unload the groceries," she said as she climbed out of her silver Volkswagen Beetle and handed me two bags from the market. I lugged them into the kitchen and set them on the counter. Inside there were a couple of giant bags of chips and avocados and salsa.

"Mmm, looks like somebody's making guacamole," I said when she came inside carrying another two big bags.

"Right you are. And Candido's going to grill burgers and hot dogs for dinner."

"Why do we need Candido for the five of us?"

"Five? Charlie says there's going to be twenty guests. Good heavens. You girls started out inviting just a few kids, and before you know it, there are twenty coming."

"Coming to what?"

"To your beach party, Doodle. Did you forget?"

"No, GoGo, I didn't forget. I never knew about it."

She stopped unpacking the groceries and stared at me. She looked puzzled.

"You mean Charlie didn't tell you about the party?"

I shook my head. Slowly, we both realized what had happened: Charlie was having a beach party. And I wasn't invited.

"I'm stunned," GoGo said softly. "When she said she was having some friends over, I just assumed she meant both of you."

"It's okay, GoGo. I have to go to rehearsal, anyway."

In some part of me, it truly was okay. I wanted to go to Truth Tellers. I knew I belonged there rather than at the SF2 party. But then why was my chin trembling, and why was my throat getting so tight? GoGo looked at me with her beautiful, sympathetic eyes, and as she walked over and put her tan arms around me, I burst into tears. She rocked me in her arms, and I just kept sobbing—sobbing for the old times when Charlie and I were two halves of a circle. I cried for wanting those old times back. And I cried for not wanting them back.

"Shhhh," GoGo whispered in my ear. "It's okay. I understand, my darling girl. Growing up is hard. It means growing apart. And that's hard. So hard."

It must have been ten minutes before I stopped crying. GoGo gave me a cold washcloth to put over my eyes so they would unpuff before I went to rehearsal. I went to our room and flopped down on my bed.

It was about an hour later when Charlie got home. I could hear her talking with Lauren in the hall, telling her to wait in the kitchen while she went in to talk to me. She looked nervous as she pushed open the door.

"So GoGo told me you know about tonight," she began.

I picked up a brush and started to brush my hair harder than was really necessary. It felt good, though, and gave me something to do so I didn't have to look Charlie in the eyes. I didn't want to cry again.

"Honestly, Sammie, it started out with just a few girls. Lauren and Brooke and Jillian and Lily and me. But then word got around, and pretty soon all the SF2s and a few other kids wanted to come. It's a great night for a beach party."

"Really? I hadn't noticed."

I picked up my bag.

"You don't have to leave, Sammie. You can be here with us. It's totally fine with me."

"That's okay. I have other plans. Besides, I would feel weird being here."

"It's your house, too. Everybody knows that."

"You guys have fun," I said. "I gotta go. We're picking up Alicia and I'm running late."

"Tell her I said hi."

"Same to Lauren."

I pulled the door open and left quickly. Thank goodness Lauren wasn't in the hall. She was the last person I wanted to see. I heard music coming from the deck, and I assumed she had gone out there to get the party started and boss everyone around.

I had to pass the deck to get to my dad's car. Without turning my head, I glanced over out of the corner of my eye and saw them. There they were, the Sporty Forty kids: Spencer, Brooke, the General, Lauren, Jillian, Jared, and all the others. Listening to music, laughing, hanging out, playing Frisbee. Just like they had been three weeks before when Charlie and I first crashed Lauren's birthday party.

Three weeks. How things had changed in three short weeks. I had a new group of friends and was going to perform onstage, something I never thought I'd do. Charlie had a new group of friends, too, and from the way she was obsessed with Spencer, maybe even a new boyfriend. It was like we had become two different people.

As I climbed into Dad's car and we drove off, I wondered if it would ever be the same again.

A Tough
Decision

....

Chapter 14

"I'm so glad you all could be here on such short notice," Ms. Carew said. We were gathered in the multipurpose room, where she had made a circle of folding chairs on the stage. She wanted us to get an idea of what it feels like to be onstage.

Duh. It feels good. Great, in fact.

"Due to a scheduling conflict, the city council has moved up the date of our performance," she went on. "We have to get right to work. No time to lose."

All the Truth Tellers were buzzing with excitement. The opportunity to perform on a big stage in front of hundreds of people was something entirely new for every one of us, and suddenly it was coming right up. We knew that the chance to talk about ourselves—our own lives, our own feelings—was an amazing opportunity to be heard and seen.

"The performance is now scheduled for this Sunday, September twenty-third, at two o'clock," Ms. Carew said. "The Santa Monica High School counselor will show a PowerPoint on drugs and teenagers, then the jazz ensemble will perform their own composition called 'Our Generation.' And we have the honor of going on last. I told them our performance is called *You Have to Be Out of Place to Find Your Place.*"

Everyone burst into applause. What a great title!

"We have enough time to do eight short pieces," Ms. Carew said. "That means some of you will have to double up."

"I can play the dentist in Keisha's piece," offered a kid named Bennett. "My dad's an orthodontist, so I've got the moves."

"That's cool with me," Keisha said.

"And I'll be the tall girl in Will's ballroom dancing piece," Sara said. "I can put my hair up on top of my head to make myself look even taller. I have a neck like a giraffe, anyway."

We got busy talking about which eight pieces we'd do and how to give everyone a chance on the stage. There were so many good ideas to pick from. We all agreed that Alicia should definitely do her cheerleading story. And I wanted to try out something I'd been working on about how it feels to be a girl who's not into fashion and—

Wait a minute. Wait a minute! Wait a minute!!!!
My mind suddenly came to a grinding halt. Did she
say September 23 at two o'clock?

My hand shot up in the air like I needed a
bathroom pass urgently.

"What is it, Sammie?" Ms. Carew asked.

"Could you repeat the date again?"

"Yes. It's this Sunday, September twenty-third, at
two o'clock in the afternoon."

My ears had heard correctly. I covered my face
with my hands.

"Do you have a problem with that date, Sammie?"

"Yeah, a big one. I can't go."

Everyone grew quiet. At last, Alicia spoke.
"Why not?"

"Diamond and Diamond versus Kozlov and Shin.
It's our first divisional tournament since we got our
ranking."

"I can't believe it," Alicia said. "The exact same
time?"

I nodded. I didn't believe it myself.

"That totally sucks," said Will. "Sorry, I mean that
totally *stinks*."

"We're in the acceptance circle, remember?"
Bernard told him. "You can say *suck* as much as
you want. Especially in this case, because Sammie's
situation doesn't stink—it *sucks*."

"You can't miss this performance," Alicia said to

me. "It's our big chance to show ourselves. Besides, I want you there."

"What choice do I have?"

"Wait, Sammie, I have a great idea," Etta said. "You could do both. Play your match with your sister, then come to the auditorium right away, in your sweaty tennis clothes and everything. You can do a really authentic piece about tennis, like how you feel out of place wearing those dorky tennis skirts. No offense."

I shook my head. "Thanks, Etta, but that's not going to work. First of all, they're called skorts. And second of all, the match will probably go two hours, maybe more."

"Two hours! We'll be at the pizza parlor by then," Keisha said. "Celebrating our successful debut. Oh . . . I'm sorry, Sammie. I didn't mean to rub it in."

"That's okay. I just wish I could be there with you guys. I've never wanted anything more—except maybe that Whoopsie Doo drink-and-wet doll for my sixth birthday that turned out to be a huge disappointment, anyway, because she only peed if you pressed her stomach really hard and then she'd leak all over her baby carriage."

I made a little chuckling sound to lighten the mood, but it didn't have much oomph.

Go ahead. Try to cheer yourself up, but it's not going to work. What you really want to do is stomp your feet and throw a total tantrum.

"Can I ask you something, Sammie?" Bernard said. "Do you even like tennis?"

It was a good question. Two months ago, I would have said, "Sure, I love tennis. Tennis is my life. Tennis is my future. My sister and I are going to be champion tennis players." But now, I wasn't so sure.

Tennis was the activity I shared with Charlie. It had been part of our lives together since we were five years old and my dad bought us our first rackets. We had spent every weekend of our lives playing tennis together. We had gone to tennis camp together. We had matching tennis outfits. She played the net and I played back. We were two halves of a circle.

But all that was changing, changing so fast that truthfully, I didn't know what I thought of tennis. I had never thought of it separately from my sister.

"I'm sorry you have a conflict, Sammie," Ms. Carew said. "But I have to know right away if you're coming. If you decide not to perform, it's only fair to give your spot to someone who wants it."

"Could I have five minutes to think it over?" I asked.

"Sure. Stay just outside the door so I know where you are."

When I got up to leave, Alicia asked if I wanted her to go with me, but I didn't. I needed to be alone to think.

I crossed the multipurpose room and stepped outside. It was still light out, but the sun was setting, so everything was starting to turn that twilight shade of lavender. I looked at the empty lunch pavilion and imagined it as it had been earlier in the day, filled with kids eating, trading sandwiches, telling jokes, and hanging out with their friends. In my mind, I saw Charlie sitting at the SF2 table, flirting with Spencer, taking delicate bites of her peach yogurt with a plastic spoon, and laughing at something silly Lauren had said. She looked so happy. Then it hit me: As I stood there imagining the scene, I didn't see myself there. I wasn't part of that table. In my mind, I had already left. Charlie was doing just fine without me.

So then why was I finding it so hard to leave Charlie behind and do what I wanted? I had two choices: go to the tennis match for Charlie or go to the Truth Tellers performance for me. Why was this so difficult? It hadn't been difficult for Charlie.

When you need to refocus, always hydrate, Dad says. *It helps revive the brain.*

I walked to the water fountain and took a long drink.

It didn't work, though. The only thing that hydrating helped me do was splatter water completely down the front of my shirt.

Should I play or perform? The question kept circling around in my head, and no clear answer was presenting itself. I thought of calling GoGo to discuss the situation. I reached for my phone, but put it back in my pocket almost immediately. There was no point in calling, because I already knew what she would say.

Follow your heart, Sammie darling. That's the only sure path to happiness I know.

Well, what happens when your heart doesn't know what to do? What then? My heart was so busy beating up a storm that I couldn't hear anything it was saying except *lub dub, lub dub, lub dub.* And frankly, that wasn't much help.

I decided to use logic, something that is not necessarily one of my talents. Logically, the main reason to choose the tennis match over the performance was Charlie. She was counting on me, and I owed it to her to show up for our match. I had to be loyal to her.

That does it; decision made. I'm going to march right in there and tell Ms. Carew I can't make the performance.

But wait. Didn't I owe it to myself to do what I wanted to do? Charlie had. She purposely didn't tell me about the party. Where was her loyalty to me?

That does it; decision made. I'm going to march right in there and tell Ms. Carew I will definitely be there for the performance.

But I had to tell Charlie right now. That was the decent thing to do. I would explain that just like her, I had found a group of friends who I wanted to be with. She would understand that. My dad wouldn't, and he'd be steaming mad. But eventually, he'd get used to the idea. GoGo would help him see my side of things.

Done. Decided. Do it.

I reached for my phone and texted Charlie.

CALL ME RIGHT AWAY. HUGE CHANGE OF PLANS. MUST TALK TO YOU.

I waited for a few minutes, but when she didn't text me back, I went into the multipurpose room. Everyone turned to look at me as I entered. I raised both my hands above my head and threw them a double thumbs-up. It was a classic GoGo move, and it made me think of her every time I did it.

"I'm in!" I shouted.

"Sam-*mie*, Sam-*mie*, Sam-*mie*," Alicia chanted, and the others joined in. It felt great to be part of such a supportive group of friends. I didn't even have to win a tournament to be accepted by them. I just had to show up.

As I was taking my seat, my phone rang. I checked the number, and it was Charlie.

"I'll be back in a second," I said. "I have to let my sister know."

I grabbed my phone and ran outside into the lunch area.

"Charlie," I said. "I'm so glad you called. I have something really important to tell you."

"Sammie," she interrupted. She was crying. "Something terrible has happened."

Did she know? Who told her?

"Charlie, hear me out first."

"Sammie, listen to me. It's GoGo."

My heart started to thump in my chest. "What's wrong with GoGo?"

"There was a car accident," Charlie said. "She's in the hospital."

"Is she okay? Please, Charlie. Say that she's okay."

All she said was, "We don't know yet. We're coming to pick you up now."

And then the phone went dead.

The Hospital

....

Chapter 15

"Where's the emergency room?" my dad asked the attendant as we came screeching into the parking lot of the Santa Monica–UCLA Medical Center. Charlie and I were in the backseat, and Ryan was sitting up front with Dad.

"You have to park in the structure," the attendant said.

"You don't understand," my dad argued. "My mother-in-law was just brought here by ambulance. We have to get to her immediately."

"Everybody's got problems here," the attendant said. "That's why it's a hospital. Park in the structure. Two lefts, then a right."

It felt like forever before we got a parking space. I was so nervous, my hands were shaking and sweating at the same time. We didn't know much—only that GoGo had left Charlie's beach party to go to the market to get more drinks. She was turning onto Pacific Coast Highway, and another car plowed into her. When the paramedics called my dad, they said she was conscious, but they didn't know the extent of her injuries.

"Why did she have to go to the store?" Charlie kept saying over and over on the drive to the hospital. "Why did she have to go?"

But of course GoGo had to go. She always wanted to make sure everyone had a good time. She wouldn't have wanted them to run out of things to drink.

The waiting room was full of people. Some were coughing, some were holding crying babies, and some were just sitting there looking sick or sad. We rushed to the reception desk where a nurse was filling out forms.

"We're here for Phyllis Platt," my dad said. "She was brought in about a half hour ago."

"Are you family?" the nurse asked.

"She's our grandmother," I blurted out. "Do you know if she's okay?"

"She's in surgery, honey. You can all take a seat in the waiting room. The doctor will speak to you when we know more."

Surgery! Oh no. What were they doing to her?

"Can you tell us anything?" Charlie asked. She sounded as scared as I felt.

"I'm sorry, dear. Only the doctor can tell you about her condition." The nurse looked at Charlie, then at me. "You're twins, right?"

We nodded.

"Which one's older?" she asked, but her phone rang before we could answer.

We took a seat where the other people were waiting and sat there for what seemed like forever. No one said a word. We were each deep in our own thoughts, too scared to talk. I knew that if Alicia were here, I'd be talking to her. Or any of the other Truth Tellers for that matter. They weren't afraid to talk about their feelings, to admit their fears. But it wasn't the Diamond family way. We were jocks. We kept our cool. We didn't show weakness. And so we were silent.

Finally Dad got up and went to the bathroom, and when he came out, he said, "You kids wait here. I'm going to call your mother. Get me right away if the surgeon comes out."

The man next to us was watching TV really loud, a show about fishermen who catch crabs. No kidding. They actually make shows about stuff like that. I couldn't take it anymore.

"Let's move," I whispered. "The TV is driving me nuts."

We got up and found three seats together. Ryan started to sit in the middle, but Charlie asked if she could sit next to me. She was looking so sad. Crying had made her eye makeup run down her face, and her nose was red from blowing it. Ryan was trying to tough it out, but he looked so pale and serious. He was always the life of the party, but now he looked like he was on the verge of crying. He picked up a magazine from the coffee table, then put it down. Picked up another one and put it down. His knee was bobbing up and down like it had a motor in it.

"She's going to be fine," he said to us. "She has to be."

"I feel so awful," Charlie said. "Oh, Sammie, if only I hadn't had that stupid party. We would have been together, just the five of us. And GoGo wouldn't have gone out for drinks, and then that stupid car wouldn't have . . ."

Her voice broke in the middle of the sentence. I reached out and took her hand.

"It's not your fault, Charlie. It was an accident."

"I just wish I could turn back the clock," she said. "I wish it were still this afternoon. I wish Mom were here."

I put my arms around her and hugged her. I could feel her trembling.

"Shhh," I whispered, like GoGo would have if she were there with us. "It's going to be okay."

"Listen, guys," Ryan said. "We have to be brave. The last thing Dad needs is three babies on his hands."

I felt my phone vibrate and reached into my purse to get it. It was Alicia.

"Do you know anything yet?" she asked.

"We're still in the waiting room. She's in surgery."

"Do you want me to come there and sit with you? My dad said he'd take me."

"It's okay. My brother and sister are here."

"Everyone from Truth Tellers says to send you big hugs. Call me as soon as you hear anything."

"I will, Alicia. Thanks for being there."

"She's a good friend," Charlie said as I put my phone back in my purse. "Solid. It's nice to have someone to lean on. Someone you can trust."

"Has Lauren called you?" I asked her.

"Not yet. I'm sure she will, though."

"She called me," Ryan said. "On the way in." He must have noticed Charlie's shocked reaction because he quickly added, "She says to send you her love and all that other girl stuff."

That was so like Lauren. She had time to call Ryan, but no time to call the girl who was supposed to be her best friend. She was what Mom calls a "boy's girl," someone who would cancel a date with a girlfriend if a boy called and asked her out. I wondered why Charlie didn't see that. I guess she just wanted to be friends with Lauren so badly, she was willing not to see the truth.

The double doors at the end of the waiting room flew open, and a doctor wearing green scrubs and a flowered surgical cap came out.

"Is the Platt family here?" she called out.

"We're here," Ryan answered, springing to his

feet so fast, he looked like a jack-in-the-box. "Actually, we're the Diamond family, but we're the Platt family, too."

Charlie bolted outside to get Dad while Ryan calmed himself down enough to explain to the doctor that our last name was Diamond, but GoGo was our mom's mom and her last name was Platt. By the time he finished, Dad and Charlie had arrived.

"How is she?" Dad asked the doctor.

I took a deep breath and braced myself for the news. Charlie reached out and took my hand.

"I'm Dr. Memsic," the surgeon began, pulling off her cap. I was surprised to see that she had long, blond hair and looked kind of like a surfer. I don't know what I thought surgeons looked like, but I thought they looked glamorous only on TV. "Ms. Platt suffered a broken tibia and fibula in the accident. Those are the bones in your shin," she explained, looking at Charlie and me.

I knew that. When you're a competitive athlete, you get very familiar with all the different bones you can break and muscles you can injure and tendons you can pull. Compared to other kids our age, the Diamond kids have a pretty complete medical vocabulary, at least as far as sports injuries go.

"We've repaired the break using four screws and a rod," Dr. Memsic went on. "As far as we can assess, aside from some bruising and cuts, that is the extent of her injuries. She'll need a few days in the hospital and six to eight weeks of recovery. Then physical therapy. But with good care, she'll be okay."

She'll be okay!!!! Oh, those were the best three words in the English language. Well, actually the best three and a half, if you count the contraction as a half.

Charlie and I fell into each other's arms, sobbing. I was so relieved that I wanted to cry and holler at the same time.

There should be a word for that. *Croller.* Yeah, that's it. I wanted to croller.

Actually, I did croller. Right in Charlie's ear. But that was okay, because she was crollering in mine!

"Now, which one of you is Sammie and which one is Charlie?" Dr. Memsic asked, looking at Ryan and Dad.

"I'm Sammie," I said. "Short for Samantha."

"And I'm Charlie. Short for Charlotte."

Dr. Memsic smiled. "Twins?" she asked. We nodded and waited for her to ask which one was older, but she didn't. Instead she said, "How's it feel to be monozygotic?"

"Huh?" Charlie and I said in unison.

"Monozygotic. That's the scientific term for *identical.* It means 'formed from one egg.'"

That was news to me. Imagine, all these years being an identical twin and the word *monozygotic* had never come up.

"Your grandmother specifically asked for you two," Dr. Memsic said. "She's in the recovery room.

She said it was important, so I'm going to let you visit for two minutes. Keep it brief and stress-free."

Dad and Ryan went outside to call Mom and tell her the good news, while Charlie and I followed Dr. Memsic through the double doors and down a gleaming, white hallway to the recovery room. At first, I gasped when I saw GoGo. She was lying in a big hospital bed with a blue oxygen tube in her nose. She was hooked up to a monitor that showed every beat of her heart, and her leg was all splinted up. Her eyes were closed, and for a minute I thought she might be dead.

"Oh, GoGo," Charlie cried. "Poor GoGo."

"Can she hear us?" I asked Dr. Memsic.

"She's still very sleepy, but she'll respond if you touch her."

Charlie and I went to GoGo's bedside and picked up her hand gently. My hand was under hers and Charlie's was over hers. It was like we were having a soft, sweet, three-way handshake.

"We're here, GoGo," I whispered.

"And we love you so much," Charlie added.

GoGo opened her eyes. She looked around the room as if she weren't quite sure where she was. Then her eyes focused on us and she smiled—that perfect, wonderful GoGo smile.

"My girls," she said, trying to sit up. "My darling girls."

Dr. Memsic came up to the bedside. "I need

you to rest now, Ms. Platt. Don't try to move. Your granddaughters can come back tomorrow."

"I have something to say," GoGo said, "and it can't wait." With that, she turned her head and focused her blue eyes on Charlie and me. "You girls were fighting," she said. "That's not good."

"We're not fighting anymore," Charlie said. "We're all better now. Aren't we, Sammie?"

Were we? I didn't know, but this was not the time to discuss it.

"All better," I said.

"You're family to each other," GoGo whispered to us, her voice sounding weak and raspy. "Family forgives. Family loves."

"We know," Charlie reassured her. "We'll fix it."

"Promise?"

"I promise," I said.

She turned to look at Charlie. "You too?"

"We're fine now. Everything is back to normal. We're playing our first divisional on Sunday, and we're going to win it for you, GoGo. Together. Isn't that right, Sammie?"

GoGo looked at me and waited for my answer. Sunday, the day of the performance. Sunday, the day of the tournament.

Which would it be?

There was no doubt in my mind now.

"We're going to win it for you, GoGo," I said.

She smiled, and as she closed her eyes and drifted off to sleep, she squeezed both our hands and whispered, "Family is love."

When we got home later that night, I took my phone into the bathroom where Charlie couldn't hear me and dialed Alicia's number.

"My grandma's okay," I said to her. "She broke her leg, but she'll recover."

"Thank God, Sammie. My whole family lit candles for her."

"Tell everyone, will you? And tell them I'm not going on Sunday."

"Because you're going to stay with your grandma?"

"No, because I'm going to play in the tournament with my sister."

There was a long silence, and then Alicia said, "Sammie, are you sure that's what you want to do?"

"My family is counting on me," I told her. And before I could start to cry, I said a quick good-bye and hung up.

The Divisionals

....

Chapter 16

"Your mom just texted that her flight gets in at seven thirty this evening," my dad said as we piled our rackets and tennis bags into the trunk of the car. "Too bad she'll miss your match."

It was Sunday afternoon, and we were heading for the tournament. A low fog hung over Santa Monica, and even though it wasn't really cold, Dad made us wear warm-up suits so our muscles would stay loose.

"Dad, she's not coming back to watch us play tennis," Charlie pointed out. She tossed the last of her things in the trunk and slammed it shut. "She's coming to see GoGo."

"A person can do two things at the same time," he said. He opened the back door of the car for us to get in. "You girls going to have enough room back there?"

"Sure," Lauren said. "We'll squeeze."

That's right. I said Lauren.

She had invited herself along to watch our match, supposedly to support us, but it just so happened that Ryan was coming, too. Aren't we all so surprised?

"Charlie, you sit in the middle because you're the smallest," Lauren ordered. I don't know who put her in charge of the seating arrangements.

Oh, right. She put herself in charge, like she did for most things.

"I'll scrunch in back of you, Mr. Diamond," she went on. "Sammie, do you think you can fit in back of Ryan on the passenger side?"

"I'm not a whale, Lauren. You don't have to strap me on top of the car or anything."

"I didn't mean to insult you. I was just saying—"

"Sammie doesn't like to talk about her size," I heard Ryan whisper as he took Lauren's hand and guided her into the backseat. "She's sensitive about it."

In the interest of keeping the peace before the tournament, I decided to let it go, although what I wanted to say was that my body's shape and size was not a topic open for public discussion. Or for private discussion, either. But recognizing that all our nerves were a little shot from the stress of the accident, I held my tongue. We had spent most of the day before at the hospital visiting GoGo. Each of us could only go in for a few minutes at a time. On each of Ryan's trips in, he'd tell her a joke from his vast collection of marginally funny jokes. On each of Charlie's trips in, she'd sing one of GoGo's favorite Beatles songs that she had taught us from the time we were born. I'm not what you'd call a great singer, so after a couple attempts at "Hey Jude," GoGo asked if I would read to her instead.

I had brought my backpack to the hospital to do homework, so all I had to read were my schoolbooks. I didn't think she'd want to hear about the causes of the American Revolution or about cell reproduction. But then I found that sheet with the Sonya Sones poem "Fantabulous," and I read it to GoGo.

"Oh, Sammie," she said. "How lovely. Read it again."

I did. I read it again and again and again, each time I went in to see her. It seemed to make her so happy. By the end of the day I knew it by heart, and I felt like, even though I'd never met her, Sonya Sones was my new best friend.

By late afternoon, GoGo was tired and wanted us to go home. Our mom was coming in, and GoGo needed to rest up for her visit. Promising that we'd call her the next day right after our match, Charlie and I kissed her good-bye and the whole family left. We were totally beat when we got home, even Ryan. (It's hard work to spend the day telling unfunny jokes.) All I wanted to do was flop down on the beach and take a long nap. But such things aren't possible when you're Rick Diamond's kid and it's the day before a divisional tournament.

"Charlie and Sammie: Get yourselves a protein snack, and I'll see you on the court in fifteen," he had said not ten minutes after we had arrived back at the club.

"Dad!" Charlie and I protested. "We're totally fried."

"When the going gets tough, the tough get going," he responded as we knew he would.

But we didn't get mad at him. It was impossible to after seeing the way he had taken care of GoGo all day. He was so sweet to her, helping her out of bed, adjusting the TV in her hospital room, holding the cup while she sipped water out of a straw.

Charlie and I couldn't stop talking about it. It reminded us both of how he was when we were really little. He always took such good care of us, even when he was working all hours. He'd make us oatmeal in the morning and homemade orange juice popsicles after dinner and read to us at bedtime every night. Of course he read sports statistics, but still, he'd snuggle with us and read until we fell asleep. To this day, I can name the top five basketball free throw shooters of 2004 and tell anyone who wants to know that it's 395 feet from home plate to the center field fence in Dodger Stadium. It was only after Charlie and I started to play tennis—no, it was only after we started to show real promise as tennis players—that he turned into tough-guy dad.

Once we were all crammed into the car (I confess, it was a tight squeeze for me in the backseat), we drove down Pacific Coast Highway to the Sand and Surf Tennis Club, the home of our most recent triumph. We registered at the desk and got our assignment. Court six at two o'clock.

"Welcome to the circuit, girls," the official at the desk said. "It's quite an honor to have achieved your Under-Fourteen ranking."

"My girls are going to make their presence felt in this division," my dad said. "You'll be seeing them on the winner's board."

"We'll all be watching for that," the official said, and turned to the next family in line.

Thanks, Dad, once again for making this a no-pressure situation.

I checked the time. It was almost one o'clock. The performance at the Civic Auditorium started at two. I wondered if everyone was out-of-their-minds nervous.

Maybe I still had time to catch Alicia. I had talked to her the night before and wished her good luck, but I was feeling the need to do it again. I kept wishing I were with the Truth Tellers and not stuck out here sweating at the Sand and Surf Tennis Club.

"Will you excuse me for a sec, Dad?" I asked after we had gotten our official badges and dropped our gear in the locker room. "I have to make a call."

"Don't be long," he said. "You shouldn't be chatting with your pals now. You've got to get your game face on, get in the zone."

"It'll only take a second."

I went out into the parking lot and speed-dialed Alicia. It rang four times, and just before it went to voice mail, she picked up. She sounded out of breath.

"Alicia?"

"Sammie! I'm so glad it's you. We're just leaving to get in the car. The whole family's going. Except Ramon. He was a total brat this morning, so we're leaving him with the neighbors. How's GoGo?"

"She stood up this morning, all on her own. I mean, with a walker, but still, she's making progress."

"That's so great. Listen, Sammie, I've got to go. I wish you could be there with us. We all do."

"Not as much as I do. But I'm doing the right thing. We're dedicating our match to GoGo."

"Then you're bound to win. I'm so nervous. I mean, the city council and all! My dad is really proud. He pinned a white carnation on the lapel of his jacket. The only other time I've seen him do that is when we go to church on Christmas. I hope I don't disappoint him."

"You'll be great," I reassured Alicia. "Speak from the heart. That's all you have to do."

When I turned around, my dad was walking quickly over to me.

"Come on, Sammie. There's a court available for you to warm up on."

I followed my dad to one of the practice courts where Charlie was doing stretches against the fence and Ryan and Lauren were sitting on the bench. When we took the court and started to hit, Dad stayed on the sidelines, calling out instructions. "Move your feet, Sammie. And follow through. Don't chop at the ball. Get to the net, Charlie. Be aggressive. Don't hang back."

We practiced for about fifteen minutes. When our muscles were warm and loose, we got some water and toweled off. Then my dad went to reserve seats in the stands, Charlie went to the ladies' room, and Ryan, who had been watching us carefully from the sidelines with Lauren, nodded his head approvingly.

"You're looking sharp, Sam-I-Am," he said. "And it's a good thing. I checked out Kozlov and Shin on the next court. Shin is fast, quick hands. Kozlov, man, she's loaded with muscle. And she's got a monster serve."

"Sammie can handle her," Lauren piped up as if she knew anything about tennis. "She can match Kozlov pound for pound."

Did she say pound for pound? Yes, she did.

Okay. That did it. I had controlled my mouth long enough. It was no longer willing to take orders from me.

"Listen here, Lauren," I heard my mouth saying. "You are not entitled to comment on my weight. You are not entitled to comment on any part of my body. In fact, you are not entitled to comment at all. Am I making myself clear?"

My mouth wanted to go on, but my head told it to stop. My mouth didn't listen, though.

"You should stick to the areas you know about," I went on, "like flirting and eye shadow."

Thanks, mouth. I think you're done now. Take a rest.

"Gosh, Sammie. You don't have to get so nasty about it." Lauren pouted. "I wasn't saying you were fat. I mean, you don't look *all that* bad."

"And what's that supposed to mean, Lauren?"

"It means exactly what it means. Sure, you're a little on the heavy side. I'm not telling you anything new. But I wouldn't call you totally fat."

I looked at Ryan, expecting him to defend me. And he didn't let me down.

"Lauren, I think you should mind your own business and shut up now. No offense."

"What is with you people today?" Lauren said. "Everyone's so touchy."

I grabbed my stuff and left the court. I wondered what Charlie would have done if she'd heard that. Would she have taken my side or Lauren's?

There was no time to think about that. The umpire was calling our names, and the crowd was gathering in the stands on court six. I was amazed at how many more people came out to see the Under-14 matches than the Under-12 matches. Dad said they were hoping to get a glimpse of someone who might become a future Wimbledon champ.

Ryan's assessment of Kozlov and Shin was right on the money. Marjorie Shin had lightning speed and great reflexes. You could tell she was a natural athlete. Quick on her feet, totally focused, and eyes that never left the ball. Her partner, Anna Kozlov, was like a hitting machine. She just hung out at the baseline and slammed back anything you hit at her. They were probably a year older than Charlie and me and, man, were they good. We had our work cut out for us.

"What's the game plan?" I asked Charlie after we had lost the racket spin and were heading to our positions.

"I could always fake an injury and forfeit," she said. When I raised my eyebrows at that remark, she laughed. "Just kidding, Sammie. There's nothing we can do except play our game. But let's face it: Those two are going to clean our clocks."

We lost our first four games. And not just regular lost, but lost as in we never scored a point. The balls just came whizzing by, and by the time I got my racket up, they were long gone. It was clear to me that although we had earned our ranking, we were way at the bottom of our division.

A few times I looked up into the stands. Our dad was giving us his Super Focus Look, staring at us without moving, beaming us silent instructions all the way across the court. I don't know if it was my imagination, but I actually thought Lauren looked pleased. She was holding Ryan's hand and offering him consoling pats on the back. Ryan saw me looking at him, and when our eyes met, I just shrugged as if to say, *It's hopeless, dude.* But then he did a typical Ryan thing. He jumped to his feet and started yelling at the top of his lungs.

"Oh no you don't. You're not giving up. You're going to win this thing."

The people around him tried to shush him. But it took more than that to shut Ryan Diamond up. He yelled out again.

"You can win this, guys. Win it for GoGo."

Charlie looked up just as Ryan threw both his arms in the air and gave us the double thumbs-up—GoGo's signature move.

They say there is magic in words, and you know what? I believe it. When Charlie and I heard Ryan shouting GoGo's name, something clicked in each of us.

"We suck," she said to me.

"Yes, we do," I answered.

"I'm sick of it," she said.

"Me too," I answered.

"Let's do this, Sammie," she said.

"I'm with you, Charlie," I answered.

And then we started to play tennis. Real tennis. I played with all my heart, believing that we could win this match. Concentrating on each shot. Remembering GoGo and how she taught us to stick together. Recalling all that I had sacrificed to be here today. Thinking of my friends at Truth Tellers and how they were giving their all at this very moment, too.

And I said to myself, *I'm going to do this. For GoGo. For Alicia. For the Truth Tellers. For me.*

Bam! I slammed a shot right down Kozlov's line. It zoomed by her.

Yeah! There's one for you, GoGo.

Pow! I served a speedball to Shin's backhand. She couldn't touch it.

That's for you, Alicia. And all the girls who couldn't afford their cheerleading outfits.

Whoosh! I rushed the net and got there in time to hit a volley right at Shin's feet.

That's for Will Lee and short sixth-grade boys everywhere.

Plop! I hit an unbelievable drop shot that just barely dribbled over the net. Kozlov rushed for it, but missed and crashed into the net.

That's for Etta and all the girls who are brave enough to have green hair and purple hair and polka-dot hair.

As my dad would say, I was in the zone.

Charlie was working it, too, playing inspired tennis. She was keeping up with me, shot for shot.

We were too far behind to win the first set, but we

won the second, and took the third to a tiebreaker. As a grand finale, I delivered two service aces that ended the match.

Charlie and I threw our rackets in the air and ran into each other's arms.

"We did it!" she said, hugging me hard.

"We certainly did," I answered, hugging her harder.

It was like old times. We were together, perfectly in sync, two halves of a mighty circle. Wow, did that feel good.

Our dad didn't stop talking all the way home, replaying every minute of the match. He was giggling like a little kid. Ryan was taking full credit for our success, claiming to have inspired us with his words. I kept smiling at Charlie, feeling so close and connected to her, even though Lauren had placed herself in the middle of the backseat, separating us.

Our mom wasn't arriving until seven thirty that night, which gave Charlie and me plenty of time to go out for Pizza Bonding. We had so much to celebrate. Our amazing and surprising win. GoGo's recovery. Our reunion after a tough couple of weeks. Our recommitment to each other. Our friendship. Our sisterhood.

Charlie got into the shower when we got home, and Ryan and Lauren went out to the beach for a walk. I called GoGo. She couldn't talk just then, but I told the nurse to tell her we had won.

"Good for you," said the nurse. "I'm sure it will make her very happy. She talks about you girls all the time."

When Dad came out of the kitchen with a glass of orange juice, he ruffled my hair like he used to do in the old days.

"You were fierce out there today," he said. "Fire in the belly. That's what makes a champion."

"Thanks, Dad. By the way, can you drop Charlie and me off at Barone's?"

He got a funny look on his face.

"Have you discussed it with your sister?"

"What's to discuss? It's our tradition. She knows that."

He nodded. "Okay. Just tell me when you're ready."

I went to our room. Charlie was out of the shower, drying her hair with a towel.

"I'm just going to shower real fast," I told her, "but I'll be ready in five minutes max. Dad said he'll drive us."

"Sammie—"

"I know what you're going to say, Charlie, and I agree. Let's get extra cheese today. And maybe some garlic rolls. I'm down with that. We deserve it after the way we played."

"Sammie," Charlie said, draping the towel around her shoulders. "I can't go to Barone's. I have plans with Lauren."

No. I wasn't hearing this. I must've gotten something wrong.

"Excuse me?"

"I'm sorry," Charlie said. "I know we always go out for pizza. But it's Spencer's birthday, and his mom and dad have invited us all out for dinner."

"But Charlie. It's our tradition. We've never missed a Pizza Bonding."

"I know. We'll do it next time. I promise."

Next time? No, we won't do it next time. And that's because there isn't going to be a next time. Not if I have anything to say about it.

Encore!

....

Chapter 17

"Dad, can you drive me downtown right now?" I asked, hurrying out of our bedroom and into the kitchen. I hadn't even changed clothes, just threw on some sweatpants over my tennis skort.

"What's the rush?" he said with a yawn. "I thought I was taking you girls to Barone's in a while."

"Yeah, well, plans changed. I need you to drop me off at the Civic Auditorium. I have to be there, like, two hours ago."

"The Civic Auditorium?" he asked, giving me a curious look. "Why do you want to go there?"

"I'm going to a city council meeting, actually," I told him.

"Oh, right. I think there's some special program there today," he said. "Read about it in the newspaper.

Something to do with kids and adults." Then he laughed. "That doesn't narrow it down too much, does it?"

"Could we hurry, please, Dad? It's important."

"Okay. Okay. I'll get my keys."

I knew he'd do it. After the win we had delivered for him earlier, he would have driven me to Mars and back if I'd asked him to.

I didn't tell Charlie I was leaving or where I was going. What difference would it make to her? She was going with her friends. Now it was time for me to be with mine. I checked the time. It was after four o'clock. Probably the meeting was over. Probably I had missed the Truth Tellers' performance. But there was always a chance. It was worth a try.

I tapped my foot nervously as we drove the half mile or so to downtown Santa Monica. It's not much of a downtown, just a mall, a couple of hotels, the police station, and the Civic Auditorium where they hold community events like Christmas concerts and gem shows and lectures on how to recycle your plastic and glass. As we got close, I noticed that the parking lot of the Civic Auditorium still had cars in it. That was a good sign. Where there are cars, there are people.

"You can just let me off there, Dad." I pointed to the main doors where a sign read *A Dialogue with Our Kids, Presented by the Santa Monica City Council. Today, 2:00.*

"Oh, that's the thing I read about," Dad said.

"Yeah, some of my friends are in there. I'm hoping to catch them."

I hadn't told him much, if anything, about Truth Tellers since that time at the dinner table when he told me he didn't see the point of it. He hadn't ever asked about it again. So I didn't see any reason to go into why I wanted to get inside so fast. I was sure my dad, unlike Alicia's father, wouldn't have pinned a carnation on his jacket and been a proud parent in the audience. He's a great guy and all, but the truth is, if it doesn't have a bouncing ball, he's not interested.

I hopped out of the car and made a mad dash for the door.

"Call when you need a ride home," he hollered after me. Without turning around, I waved my hand to let him know I had heard him.

There was a woman sitting at a bridge table at the door. The table was covered with leaflets on various topics, from recycling to parking permits to tide charts. I sprinted toward her.

"You're a little late, honey," she said when I reached her table.

"It's not over yet, is it?"

"They're just wrapping it up, I believe. But can I interest you in some information on next weekend's craft show?"

"Is it okay if I just go in, anyway?" I asked, and before she could answer, I heard a huge cheer and a giant round of applause coming from inside the hall.

"Sounds like you just missed it, but go on in if you'd like."

I darted inside and practically galloped across the lobby. Throwing the door to the auditorium open, I saw a room full of people, all on their feet and applauding like crazy. Up on the stage, the Truth Tellers were gathered in a half circle, and standing in the middle of them all was Alicia. She was taking a bow. She smiled broadly at the audience, and I saw her look over at Candido, Esperanza, and her grandmother and blow them a kiss. Six adults, also standing and applauding, were behind a table set up onstage. There was a name tag in front of each of their places, and I assumed they were the city council members.

I wanted to scream. I was so close to getting there in time, but obviously I had just missed Alicia's performance. From the reaction she was getting from the crowd, I knew it had to have been super. I crept down the aisle to the front row, hoping to find an empty seat. Alicia spotted me as she looked up from taking her third bow. *I did it,* she mouthed.

Ms. Carew saw me, too, and flashed me a happy smile. There were no chairs, so I just scrunched down in the aisle.

"I want to thank Ms. Carew and her remarkable group of students from Beachside Middle School," one of the council members said when the applause finally died down. "Too often we talk to our kids, but we don't listen to them. I think we've learned today that these fine young people have a lot to teach us about facing challenges with courage and honesty."

The audience applauded again, and then a couple of the parents started yelling "Encore!" The crowd picked up on it, and soon lots of people were yelling "Encore! Encore!"

The councilman quieted them down with his hands, then turned to Ms. Carew.

"It appears our citizens haven't heard enough from your students," he said. "Do you have one more piece you'd like to do about life in middle school?"

Ms. Carew looked at the group assembled onstage.

"Kids? Is there something more you'd like to do?"

They talked among themselves for a second, then Alicia spoke up.

"Yes, we have one more thing," she said. "Everyone stay where you are. I'll be right back."

She bounced down the stairs of the stage, came over and got me, and pulled me back onstage with her.

"What are you doing?" I whispered.

"We've all had our turns," she said. "Now it's yours."

"I can't. I don't know what to say."

"You're a Truth Teller, Sammie. Time to tell it like it is."

"But I don't have anything prepared."

"Remember what you told me?" she said. "Speak from the heart. That's all you have to do."

Alicia deposited me in the middle of the stage, then joined the others and left me standing alone in front of the microphone, facing the largest group of people I'd ever faced . . . without a tennis racket in my hand and Charlie at my side, that is. It was scary.

I looked over at Ms. Carew. I'm sure she could see the fear in my eyes. I had no game to hide behind. No forehand or backhand. No killer serve. No strategy. No sister. Just me and my mouth and my heart.

My mind was a total blank. All those faces staring at me, waiting for me to talk. I looked down at my feet and suddenly realized that I was standing onstage in my grungy sweatpants. I felt completely embarrassed. And that gave me an idea.

"As you can see," I said into the microphone, "I'm not much into fashion. I'm a tennis player, a jock, and my idea of dressing up is sweatpants and a T-shirt. That makes me something of a geek at Beachside. I don't have great hair or made-up eyes or glossy lips like a lot of the other girls. And in case you didn't notice, I don't have a skinny, little body. It doesn't look good in tight clothes, that's for sure. But it's my body. It's strong and healthy, and I'm trying to learn to think it's . . . well . . . fantabulous."

And then, I recited Sonya Sones's poem.

"I don't need to rock
a pair of size 2 jeans
or prance through the pages
of magazines

*because I am a woman
who's round and full,
made of wind and wild
and honey.*

*A woman made
of curve and swerve
and flow and glow
and strong and funny.*

*I am a woman made
of fire and fierce and free.
I am fantabulous.
Fantabulous me!"*

When I finished, there was total silence in the room. And then one of the moms in the back row stood up and yelled, "You tell 'em, girlfriend. You tell 'em like it is!"

All the women in the room jumped to their feet and started to applaud. Pretty soon, the men followed. The whole room was standing and cheering.

And they were cheering for me.

Pizza

....

Chapter 18

"You rocked the house," Keisha said to me, stuffing a large slice of pepperoni pizza into her mouth.

"Correction. *We* rocked the house," I answered, chomping down on my own slice with olives. I had thought of ordering sausage and mushroom, but it didn't seem right. Not yet. It would take a while before I could do that.

"Can you believe the reaction we got?" Alicia giggled.

"Yes, I can," Sara said. "And do you know why we got it?"

"Because we rock!" everyone said in unison.

The Truth Tellers were gathered around a long table at Antonio's Pizza Parlor, which was just down the street from the Civic Auditorium. Ms. Carew had offered to take us all out for pizza to celebrate, and we accepted, naturally.

"I'm proud of each and every one of you," Ms. Carew said, raising a glass of lemonade to toast us. "It takes courage to tell the truth, especially to yourselves. So I salute you guys. Here's to truth and here's to pizza!"

We ate and laughed and celebrated. Just as we were polishing off the last slices, the door opened and another large group of kids came in. The General led the way, followed by Brooke. Then Jillian and Sean, Lily and Lauren, Spencer and . . . Charlie. At first she didn't see me, but when she did, she froze in place. I think I was the last person she was expecting to see.

There were eight SF2s in all. Spencer brought up the rear, and he was followed by the man who had talked at the city council meeting. When the man saw our group, he marched right over to our table.

"Congratulations again," he said, going around and shaking each of our hands. Then, turning around, he called out, "Spence, come on over here for a minute."

Spencer, who was taking a seat next to Charlie, left her side and walked over to our table.

"Do any of you guys know my son Spencer?" the man said. "Say hello to a remarkable group of kids, Spence."

"Hey, guys," Spencer said. Then, seeing me, he added, "What's up, Sammie?"

"You never told me your dad was on the city council," I said.

"You never asked. Everyone, meet my dad, Tom Ballard. Watch out, or he'll shake your hands again. Nothing he likes better than to press the flesh." Spencer slapped his dad on the back in a really sweet way, then flashed a cocky grin which I swear was aimed at me. I noticed that he had a dimple on one side when he smiled. Why hadn't I ever noticed that before?

Maybe it's because he never smiled at you before, airhead. Did you ever think of that?

"So how is it you don't know any of these kids?" Mr. Ballard asked Spencer. "You go to the same school, for crying out loud."

"I know Sammie really well," Spencer said. "She throws a mean Frisbee. She's Charlie's twin sister."

Mr. Ballard looked over at Charlie, then back at me.

"So she is," he said. "Oh, wait a minute. You're Rick's girls, from the club."

I nodded. By that time, Charlie had come over to say hi. I noticed that none of the other SF2s joined her. They were already sitting down, ordering Cokes from the waiter. Lauren was figuring out what kind of pizzas they should order. In charge, as always.

"So tell me, ladies," Mr. Ballard said, putting an arm around Charlie. "Which one of you is older?"

"I'm older," Charlie said.

"And I'm wiser," I said. And this time, I really meant it.

Mr. Ballard let out a big, friendly laugh.

"You're a hoot!" he said to me.

"So people say," I told him, nodding.

Then he shook my hand and waved good-bye to all of us. You could see how a friendly guy like that got elected to city council. He and Spencer went back to their table to join the SF2 kids. I could tell Charlie wanted to go, but she didn't. She just stood there like she was reporting for duty, looking awkward and uncomfortable.

"So where have you guys been?" she asked.

Alicia told her about our performance at the Civic Auditorium. She seemed very surprised.

"Did you go?" she said to me.

"I was supposed to, but I missed most of it. I got there at the very end."

"But just in time to be a smash," Alicia said. "You should've seen her. You would have been so proud."

I could tell Charlie was thinking, biting her lower lip like she does when she's concentrating. Our waiter brought a tray of ice-cream sundaes for dessert, and everyone lunged for them. Except me. This time, it wasn't that I was watching my weight. I was watching Charlie.

"So you skipped your show because of our tournament?" she said.

I nodded. "I promised GoGo."

"You didn't tell me about the show," she said.

"You didn't tell me about Spencer's party," I replied.

"You didn't ask."

"Neither did you."

That was the truth of it. Just a few weeks before, we would have known. About the party, about the performance, about each other. But that was before Beachside, before the SF2s, before I learned how to be a Truth Teller. Now there was a strange gap between us. Not necessarily in a bad way. But definitely in a new way.

"Well, I better get back," Charlie said. "My friends are waiting for me."

I nodded. "So are mine."

I watched her go over and take a seat between Spencer and Lauren. She looked natural there in between them, like she belonged.

I felt a hand on my shoulder. It was Alicia.

"You okay?" she asked.

I looked over at Charlie's table, then back at my own, filled with my new friends.

"You know what, Alicia? I'm more than okay," I said, taking her hands and feeling entirely like a Truth Teller. "I'm fantabulous."